# BAREFOOT IN THE CITY OF BROKEN DREAMS

## BRENT HARTINGER

BOOKS

For Michael Jensen

And for all those people crazy enough to chase
some stupid, impractical dream

# CHAPTER ONE

I was floating facedown in a swimming pool, completely motionless, dead to the world.

Down below me, along the bottom of the pool, something brown and frond-like hung in the water. Old leaves, probably. They were absolutely still, just like I was. It was like they were suspended in plastic acrylic. The water in the pool around me was completely still too. We were all frozen in time.

My name is Russel Middlebrook, I was twenty-four years old, and my life was over. I'd just moved from Seattle to Los Angeles. This was the pool in the courtyard of my new apartment building, but I was dead now, so I'd never get a chance to enjoy it.

The water moved around me. Down on the bottom of the pool, the dead leaves jerked and swirled.

Someone had climbed into the water with me, someone with hairy, muscular legs that lead up to a pair of well-packed navy trunks.

My boyfriend Kevin.

I lifted my head.

"Hey there," he said, with a grin that gave me a reason to live again.

Okay, okay, so I wasn't literally "dead." But I really had felt that way. Moving from Seattle to Los Angeles had been exhausting. First, we'd flown down to Los Angeles to rent the apartment, then back to Seattle again to pack our whole lives into boxes. Then we loaded those boxes into the moving truck and drove our car a thousand miles down to California to meet the truck. And then we did the whole damn thing in reverse, unloading and unpacking, destroying my back with all the lifting and somehow cutting my fingers to shreds on the cardboard. We'd spent the last two days unpacking, and it seemed like we'd barely started, like all we'd really done is move the boxes into the right rooms.

But being with Kevin, the guy I loved, none of that mattered. Now, for the first time in our relationship, we finally had the chance to live together. So as bad as it had been getting here, it hadn't been that bad. And in spite of being completely exhausted, I couldn't have been happier.

Here's where I'm also supposed to say: "It's not like our relationship was perfect." And, "We had our problems just like anyone else. It drove me crazy the way he squeezed the toothpaste, and I could already tell we were going to fight over how to load the dishwasher." That way, those of you who are in bad or so-so relationships will still be able to relate. And those of you who aren't in relationships at all won't be jealous.

Problem is, our relationship *was* perfect, or pretty darn near. Basically, Kevin was my hot best friend who I also got to have sex with.

In our defense, we'd had our share of problems in the past. Basically, we'd been on-again, off-again for seven years, ever since we first started dating in high school. But we'd gotten together for good the November of the previous year, and it was early September now, and things had been incredible ever since. Maybe the stress of this move to Los Angeles, or the high expectations of our finally living together after all these years, would be our undoing. Or maybe this was all just some sort of honeymoon period that would inevitably end in a flurry of broken dishes and violently squeezed toothpaste tubes.

I doubted it. Kevin was the Ennis Del Mar to my Jack Twist, but without all the self-hatred, and fewer canned beans. (These are *Brokeback Mountain* references. If you've never seen the movie, you should. Oh, and you're dead to me.)

Even so, I did feel a certain amount of guilt. I was the reason why Kevin and I decided to move to Los Angeles in the first place. He'd been happy in Seattle (more or less). But the year before, I'd met this really great old lady named Vernie Rose who had once been sort of a famous screenwriter. She'd inspired me to become a screenwriter myself. At one point, Vernie had told me that if I was really serious about it, I needed to move to Los Angeles. Kevin and I had talked it over, and we'd decided: Why not go now when we were young, before we had commitments and obligations? Besides, we were ready for a change.

Kevin sank deeper into the pool. "Why is this so damn refreshing? Back home, swimming pools are never this refreshing."

"Oh!" I said. "I just read something about that. It's the interaction between the temperature of the air and the temperature of the water. Or, wait, maybe it has to do with the lack of humidity. The heat is drier, so the water feels different."

Kevin smiled. "So basically, it feels better here. Thanks, I didn't know that."

I splashed him. Being in a perfect relationship didn't preclude our teasing each other. A lot. In fact, it was big part of what made the relationship so perfect.

A woman walked into the courtyard of our new building—the Escala Apartments. The courtyard was actually pretty dumpy: leaves in the pool, cracks in the concrete, and, yes, faded plastic plants and Astroturf in place of most of the landscaping (oy!).

"Hey, there," Kevin said to the woman.

She looked over at us, perplexed, taken aback a bit. I guess she wasn't used to people being friendly in this building, or maybe even in this city.

She was tall and bony with lots of angles—a praying mantis of a woman, except that makes her sound dangerous, and I actually liked the way she looked, that she had a bit of an edge. She had dark red hair, definitely dyed, in sort of a tight shag haircut. Her clothes had a crunchy vibe—some embroidery, a tassel or two—but I had a feeling it was misleading, like whiskers on a mountain lion. This was a woman who was clearly ready to rumble.

"We're new," Kevin said. "From Seattle? I'm Kevin." He nodded at me. "This is my boyfriend Russel."

She smiled a knowing little smile. "Gina," she said. She drifted closer to the pool. "You guys actors?"

"Editor," Kevin said, meaning himself. He was

more an editor/journalist—non-fiction only. "Russel's a screenwriter."

She gave me another knowing nod, but secretly I was sort of flattered she thought I was handsome enough to be an actor. Then again, maybe she was mostly looking at Kevin who, incidentally, really *is* handsome enough to be an actor. Or maybe it was as simple as the fact that so many people in Los Angeles are actors, or trying to be. I'd lived in Los Angeles for less than three days, but even I knew that.

"What are you?" I asked Gina, meaning, what do you do?

"Stand-up comedian," she said.

She didn't say anything else, and Kevin and I just stared at her.

"You're waiting for me to say something funny, aren't you?" she said drolly.

*Busted.* Kevin and I smiled.

"We're in 2-B," I said.

"Yeah?" Gina said, raising an eyebrow.

"Why 'yeah?'" I said. "Did someone kill themselves in our unit or something?"

"Actually, yeah," Gina said. "There's even supposed to be a ghost."

"Shut up!" Kevin said, in a way that was sort of a cross between "Yikes!" and "*Cool!*"

I looked at Kevin. "The manager didn't say anything about anyone killing themselves."

"Well, it was, like, fifty years ago," Gina said.

"So is it like that season of *American Horror Story* where they don't need to tell anyone about a death in the house if it happened more than three years before?" I said.

"It's more like he's a shitty Los Angeles landlord who doesn't give a crap what he tells you," Gina said, "because he knows there'll always be someone else to come along and rent it if you don't."

"Why'd he kill himself?" Kevin asked. "'He'?"

She nodded. "Think so. And why does anyone ever kill themselves in Hollywood? Failed actor or failed writer—can't remember which. Which is funny. You never hear about the ghost of someone who moves to Hollywood to become a key grip, but doesn't get the job and ends up killing himself."

Kevin and I laughed.

"You *did* say something funny," I said. "Just not right away."

"Performance anxiety."

"So about this ghost..." Kevin said, in a tone that was only half-serious. "Is that why the previous tenant left?"

"Sort of. The ghost murdered her. That actually *was* like that season of *American Horror Story*." But Gina was smiling when she said this, so I knew she was joking. "The truth is, I don't think there's a single hotel or apartment in all of Los Angeles that isn't sup-posedly haunted by the ghost of someone who killed themselves after their dreams were crushed. Trust me on this, I've lived in a *lot* of old buildings."

I smiled again. At the same time, I looked at Gina, trying to guess her age. Mid-forties, maybe?

"Anyway," she said, turning to go. "Nice to meet you guys."

\* \* \*

Once we'd showered and dressed, it was late afternoon, so we decided to walk some place for dinner. We'd been in town two full days, but we'd been inside almost the whole time. We'd barely even seen our own neighborhood.

We stepped out onto the sidewalk, into the city, all fresh-faced and naive.

Our apartment was halfway up a hill. Behind us, a half block away, was the Hollywood Freeway, which I would soon learn is also called the 101, but never on the same sign. In other words, the freeway has two different names, but the city doesn't bother to tell you—you're somehow just expected to know. Likewise, I'd eventually learn that the Arroyo Seco Parkway is also called the 110, and sometimes the Pasadena Freeway, but no one ever tells you that either.

Meanwhile, in front of us, Los Angeles stretched out forever. That's the way it looked anyway: this endless expanse of city that rolled on and on, eventually disappearing into the smoggy brown smear of eternity. Closer in, down below us, you could make out the buildings and streets and palm trees, but farther on, all the concrete started to sort of blur together, making the city look like this vast plane of jagged gravel. Los Angeles actually has a pretty impressive downtown to the southeast of where we were, with skyscrapers and everything, and there are these other clusters of skyscrapers on the horizon too, but none of them looked all that impressive from here, because everything was so spread out, and even the tall buildings got lost in the expanse and the smog.

We headed down the hill, toward the main drag. We passed more apartment buildings like our own, some nicer than ours, but most even dumpier. Los Angeles smelled totally different from Seattle: a weird mix of rubber, asphalt, and car exhaust that would be completely unbearable without the hint of salt from the sea, and the honeysuckle and jasmine from the Hollywood Hills behind us.

One street over, a tall, cylindrical building rose up over the rooftops.

"Oh!" I said. "The Capitol Records Tower! You know, from the opening scene in *Hancock*, when Will Smith impales the robbers' car on the spire on top?"

Kevin smiled, totally humoring me.

I should get this out of the way right now: I love movies. I've loved them for as long as I can remember. (Full disclosure: I'm done with the super-hero thing. It was fun for a while, but now they all seem the same. And besides, sequels, reboots, and remakes are basically the death of originality, as any writer will tell you.) Anyway, I know my insane love for movies pretty much makes me a Big Gay Cliché, but sometimes the stereotypes are right, and there's something to be said for just owning it. In fact, as stressful as our move to Los Angeles had been, I'd been really excited to become part of the filmmaking capital of the world, and also to see the locations of all my favorite movies. (Which isn't to say that *Hancock* is one of them. Let's just say I may have boned up on trivia about all the movie locations in our neighborhood on the roadtrip down.)

Right before we reached Hollywood Avenue, we passed one of the buildings for the Church of Scientology—that screwed up Hollywood religion that Tom Cruise is a member of? Supposedly, it's like a cult, and they lure you in and prey on your insecurities, brainwashing you into giving them all your money, and they blackmail you with details about your private life if you don't pay up.

There was a big red banner on the wall of the building that said, "All are welcome!"

"What do you think?" I said to Kevin. "Should we go in?"

"Um, yeah," Kevin said. "No, thanks."

"Seriously, though, don't you want to know how they do it? Don't you feel like, whatever they do, it couldn't possibly work on you? That you're too smart to be brainwashed?"

"Okay," Kevin said, starting toward the door. "Let's go in."

I laughed, stopping him. "I don't want to know *that* much! It's like how they claim if you say 'Bloody Mary' three times in a row into a mirror, the ghost of Bloody Mary will appear. No one really thinks that, but no one ever wants to test it either."

Finally, we came to Hollywood Boulevard.

"I can't believe it!" I said. "Our apartment is six blocks from Hollywood and Vine."

"What?" Kevin said.

I pointed. "One block down. That's Hollywood and Vine."

"Okay," Kevin said, humoring me again. "What do you have to tell me about Hollywood and Vine?"

"Nothing," I said, but I was almost quivering I was so excited. "Nothing at all."

"Really?"

"No, not really!" I said, bursting open like the dam in *Dante's Peak.* "Hollywood and Vine was the very first intersection in Hollywood, before Hollywood even existed, when the first orchard owner subdivided her land! A couple of decades later, it had become the center of the whole industry, with all the farms and orchards turned into movie lots, and all the movie studios having their headquarters right along this road!"

Kevin glanced around the block we were on. I had to admit it wasn't much to look at now: a tattoo parlor, a payday loan place, a couple of boarded up storefronts, and an actual strip club.

"The movie studios aren't here anymore," I said. "They're spread out all over the city. Now this is the tourist-y part of the town. Look, here's the Hollywood Walk of Fame." I pointed to the sidewalk along Hollywood Boulevard where pink marble stars had been set into black marble squares, each one with a name and little symbol indicating whether the "star" was a star of movies or TV or whatever. There was dried gum and bird crap all over the place, but still.

"The Chinese Theatre is only a few blocks that way," I went on, pointing away from Hollywood and Vine, "along with the Egyptian, and the El Capitan, and Madame Tussaud's Wax Museum, and that weird sculpture of the four silver women. What's that called anyway? Does it even have a name?"

"The Gateway to Hollywood," Kevin said.

I frowned. Kevin liked movies too (including— *groan*—superhero movies), but only as a casual fan. Earlier that year, he hadn't known who Jimmy Stewart was (how is that even *possible*?). So how in the world did he know something I didn't?

"I'm not a complete idiot," he said.

"Name three celebrities who have left an imprint in the concrete in front of the Chinese Theatre."

He looked at me blankly.

*And the cosmic scales are righted!* I thought.

Feeling way too smug, I led Kevin down Hollywood Boulevard, in the direction of the Chinese Theatre. Technically, we were looking for a place to eat, but I was mostly taking in all the sights. From the street, I could see the famous white "Hollywood" sign up in the hills to our right. I was also reading the names on the different stars in the sidewalk. (Fun fact: there are actually two Harrison Fords on the Walk of Fame. There's the guy everyone knows, and also a silent film star who everyone's now forgotten.)

Kevin and I hadn't *intended* to get an apartment so close to Old Hollywood—not even me, lover of all things Hollywood. In fact, we'd originally tried to find a place in West Hollywood (and not just because it's so gay, also because it's really nice).

Incidentally, if you don't already know this, West Hollywood is an entirely different town from Hollywood, which actually isn't a "town" at all (it merged with the city of Los Angeles in 1910). So to clarify: West Hollywood is an actual incorporated city, but Hollywood is just one vague geographic part of Los Angeles, and also sort of a catch-all term for the movie industry in general.

Unlike the crazy business with the different freeway names, I actually think the difference between Hollywood and West Hollywood is pretty interesting, but let me know if I'm boring you.

So anyway, there Kevin and I were, exhausted from moving and starving because we'd been too lazy to even pop something into the microwave.

I looked down at the names on the stars on the Walk of Fame again.

Anne Bancroft!

Richard Pryor!

Graham McNamee!

*Who the hell is Graham McNamee?* I thought. But I wasn't about to ask Kevin for fear that he might possibly know something else I didn't know.

This is also a total cliché, but I couldn't help thinking: *Will my name be engraved on a star on this sidewalk one day?*

Still taking it all in, overwhelmed by everything around me, I stopped. It was like history was a river, and I'd stepped right into it, and now it was flowing all around me. I had spent the last couple of years of my life completely adrift, with no purpose, no direction. But now I had an anchor, something to cling to: I was determined to make it as a screenwriter.

That was the whole point of this move to Los Angeles. Would I achieve my dreams? Would I ever actually become part of the river of Hollywood history? Would I somehow change the course of this town, even a little bit? Or would the river flow right through me, ignoring me, as if I'd never even been there at all? I knew I couldn't go back to my old life of no direction—that was just too pathetic for words. For me, it was Hollywood or bust. (But what exactly did it mean when someone went bust in Hollywood? Were they broken?)

I thought about all the movies I'd seen about Hollywood: *The Bodyguard, Barton Fink, Singin' in the Rain, The Player, Adaptation, A Star is Born,* and on and on. In those films, the main character always comes to town, wide-eyed and innocent, and before they know it, they're forced to choose between Massive Hollywood Success or Their Soul. I know I literally just said a few paragraphs ago that I was fresh-faced and naive, but I knew that wouldn't ever happen to me. After all, I'd already seen all those movies. I knew how things worked. I'd never give up *my* soul. (On the other hand, it was a little like that Scientology Building: I was certain I'd never fall for their brainwashing, but I also wasn't entirely sure I wanted to be tested.)

"What is it?" Kevin asked me.

"Nothing," I said, starting forward again. I'm trying not to bore you here, and I didn't want to bore Kevin then either.

"Russel?" Kevin said, stopping me. "It's all good. I think this stuff is interesting."

I looked at him. "It's just that we're really here. We *live* here. In *Hollywood*." Technically, Los Angeles.

Living in L.A. wasn't new for Kevin. He'd gone to college at UC Irvine, and even if he hadn't spent a lot of time in "Hollywood" per se, he'd been here. He knew the city, even the right names for all the freeways. But I didn't. He looked at me, then he looked around, a really good look, at the buildings, at the stars on the Walk of Fame, as if seeing it all through my eyes.

That made me smile.

"Thanks," I said.

He looked back at me. "For what?"

"For doing this for me."

"I'm not doing it *for* you. I'm doing it *with* you. We're a team now."

I was bursting again, even more than before—like the Hoover dam in the original *Superman* (very cheesy-looking, but a much bigger flood than *Dante's Peak*). This time I was bursting with emotion.

I leaned forward and kissed Kevin right there on the sidewalk. Somehow I knew intuitively that no one in Los Angeles would look twice at two guys kissing. But we were in the tourist-y part now, full of people from North Dakota and Arkansas, so we did draw a couple of double-takes.

Kevin didn't just kiss me back. He pulled me into him, a long, passionate embrace, exactly like, well, two characters kissing in a movie (but probably not two men, because honestly, even now, how often do you see two men kiss in the movies?).

The point is, it was incredibly romantic. A couple of teenage girls actually clapped. When we finally pulled apart again, I was a little surprised that Los Angeles was still standing. It seemed like everything should have collapsed around us in an earthquake.

I'd like to say the evening went on like that, totally romantic, still like in some movie—that we had a candlelight dinner on the sidewalk table of some charming little bistro, then we held hands as we meandered through cobblestone alleys strung with fairy lights, finally ending up back in our apartment where we had perfectly-lit sex, alternately gentle and a little rough, just enough to shock and titillate Middle American movie audiences.

The truth is, we had dinner at Popeye's (oy!), and then proceeded to get lost. I'd heard it said that no one ever walks in L.A., and I was quickly learning why. Everything was too spread out, and the cars were openly hostile to pedestrians—and I mean openly hostile in the sense that they actively try to run you down if you inconvenience them, and sometimes even if you look at them wrong. Finally, we asked for directions from the bouncer at another strip club (he had terrible breath).

But all this makes sense, right? This isn't the plot to some movie.

Even then, Kevin and I never got impatient with each other. Every time something went wrong, we just laughed it off. And we did end up having pretty hot sex that night.

So I take back what I said before: even with the scary drivers, and the equally scary breath of that strip club bouncer, the whole night was still totally romantic.

Ordinarily, I fall asleep after sex (like most guys). But I was too keyed up that night. So after Kevin dropped off to sleep (like most guys), I found myself awake in the dark, staring at the shadows on the ceiling and listening to the sounds of the city at night outside our open window: the hiss of the freeway, the grind of an automatic garage door opener, the swoosh of a car on the street just outside followed by the clatter of dried leaves.

Before too long, I decided to get up. I've always been a night owl—when the sun goes down is when I feel most alive. I didn't turn on the lights in the main room. I couldn't bear to see all that we still had left to do, the boxes yet to be opened. I sank down into the couch in my t-shirt and underwear.

There was something about my senses then, how alive I felt. First, walking down Hollywood Boulevard with Kevin, feeling the history of the city, now being alone in our new apartment in the dark—I wanted to drink it all in, feel it seeping into me, becoming a part of me. It was scary, living in a city where I didn't know a single person other than Kevin, but it was exciting too, like jumping off a cliff and not knowing what was at the bottom: rocks, or water, or maybe nothing at all, just air and clouds for all eternity.

That, of course, is when I remembered the ghost that supposedly haunted our apartment, the one Gina had told us about earlier. I wasn't truly scared, even sitting in the dark like that. I don't believe in ghosts. Or UFOs. Or ESP. Interestingly, I do kinda sorta believe in Bigfoot, but that's a whole other story.

Anyway, I was sitting in the dark of that apartment, looking around the room. Ghosts may not be real and—let's face it—the story behind the ghost, the guy who supposedly killed himself in our apartment fifty years earlier, that might not have been real either.

But that apartment was more than fifty years old (and so was the plumbing, trust me). In all those years, lots of people must have lived in the room where I was sitting. Given that this was Hollywood— so close to the *actual* Old Hollywood—that meant that over the years, plenty of those occupants probably *had* been actors and writers (and maybe even a few key grips).

I couldn't help but think about all those people. Had any of them gone on to become stars? Had any great screenplays been written here? Part of me thought that if Chris Hemsworth or Mila Kunis had ever lived in this apartment building, or if *Casablanca* or *Up in the Air* had been written here, Kevin and I would know. The landlord would have bragged about it, or Gina would have said something. Hell, there'd probably even be a plaque like there was on one of the neighboring buildings that said Fatty Arbuckle and Claudette Colbert once lived there.

So what did it mean that no one had said anything? That in all these years, with all these thousands of people moving in and out of the Escala Apartments, no one ever had become a star? No writers had ever been inspired to write any great movies?

That was impossible. Wasn't it?

As I sat there in the dark, my mind began to wander.

*A woman paces, script in hand, memorizing lines for an audition, even as she knows she'll also have to rehearse what she'll tell the landlord if she doesn't get this part and isn't able to pay the rent again.*

*A screenwriter, a cigarette dangling from his lips, sits at his typewriter, keys clacking, determined to ignore the ever-rising stack of unsold screenplays on the bureau behind him.*

*A man in his late twenties stares at himself in the mirror by the door, knowing that he should probably pick a different tie, but starting to think it won't make any difference—that the mailroom isn't just the place where he started, it's also the place where he'll end up.*

Talk about ghosts from the past!

Had any of the people who lived in this apartment been gay couples like Kevin and me? Since I was sitting there in the dark in my underwear, I couldn't help but wonder if they were hot, if maybe they'd ever had hot sex right in the area in front of me. Maybe it had even been discreet, clandestine gay sex, which is terrible, because it would have been the result of all the prejudice and discrimination of the era, but at that particular moment, even thirty minutes after just having sex with Kevin, it was undeniably hot.

*A handsome young actor, returning from his audition in a dark suit and narrow tie, enters the apartment, exhaling in relief, finally able to take off the mask of his daily charade. His "roommate," a strapping stuntman in a lumberjack shirt, meets him at the door with a passionate embrace, his hands quickly slipping under a tightly-notched buckle and binding elastic. The actor's trousers fall down around his ankles in a satisfying* whoosh, *and the stuntman is on his knees in front of him, taking the actor's straining cock into his mouth.*

All these people—the actress, the screenwriter, the mailroom guy, the horny gay couple—they were surprisingly vivid, at least in my mind. I could almost *see* them. I thought of myself as a pretty good writer, but creating characters, the people in my screenplays, had never come this easily to me before.

*Maybe this isn't my imagination,* I thought. Maybe these were real people, the people who had actually lived in this apartment over the years. Maybe I was somehow peering through the veils of time and seeing things as they really were in the years and decades before.

I kept watching them, these ghosts in my mind, and other ghosts appeared around me too.

*A weary man returns from yet another rejection, hungry, wishing they'd at least invited him into the commissary for one good meal of the day.*

*A screenwriter punches a wall, certain his idea has been stolen, knowing that somehow someone at that studio had read his script, but also knowing there was no way he could ever prove it.*

*A matronly woman pleads with the young woman with the tear-stained face to pack her bags, give up her foolish dreams, and come home with her.*

(I admit I also kept seeing the handsome actor and

the stunt man, who had moved on from cock-sucking to, um, more. And don't get me started on the married studio executive in the pin-striped suit who had finally come to see the apartment of his fresh-faced personal assistant!)

My mind swam, overwhelmed by all the emotion surrounding me—the struggle, the pain, the passion.

But after ten minutes or so, the ghosts of the past started to fade, and the wash of sleep finally arrived.

I stood up and went back into the bedroom and climbed onto our futon. Maybe it was the romantic night we'd had, or maybe it was the lingering memory of all those hot 1950s ghosts fucking in the front room (or maybe it was a little of both), but I cuddled up next to Kevin, who, even barely awake, immediately noticed I had a boner. We started kissing and soon we were having sex again—hot, middle-of-the-night sex.

There had been ghosts back in that living room, real or imagined, but I had left them behind. I didn't feel dead or even exhausted anymore, the way I'd felt floating out in the pool earlier. In fact, I felt totally alive, the opposite of the ghosts of our apartment, sexy or not. Our move to Los Angeles had been a drag (the actual move, I mean). But now that we were here, I couldn't wait for the adventure to begin. I knew there was absolutely nothing Los Angeles could throw at me that I couldn't throw right back.

As I was lying there in the dark, a question occurred to me: *What if I don't have the slightest idea what I'm talking about?* But I'd just had more great sex, and this time I did fall right asleep (like most guys), so I didn't get a chance to finish the thought.

# CHAPTER TWO

I take back what I said before, that I didn't know any-one in Los Angeles. I actually did have one friend, Otto Digmore, and I was meeting him for lunch the very next day.

Otto and I had met at summer camp back when I was sixteen. He and I actually ended up boyfriends. Yes, yes, cue all the share-a-sleeping-bag and circle jerk summer camp jokes, but it wasn't like that. Well, okay, it sort of was, but that's not the point. We'd actually been in love, and we stayed boyfriends after camp too. But he lived in California, and I was back in Washington State, and the long-distance thing didn't really work out for us, so we eventually broke up.

Otto and I tried hard to stay friends, chatting on-line, buying birthday gifts from each other's wish lists. But since we'd broken up, I'd only seen him twice in person: once when I went to Disneyland with my family, and once when I visited Kevin at school. We were still in touch, liking each other's posts, but we didn't really "talk." I couldn't remember the last time we'd even chatted.

In other words, by this point, Otto and I were mostly just Facebook friends.

So *did* I have a friend in Los Angeles? I mean, Otto probably had his own circle of friends now, a whole Los Angeles life that was all set up and running, like one of those elaborate train models you see at Christmas, everything glued into place. Would there be room for me in his perfect Bavarian village? Or, hey, maybe he'd changed since summer camp. Maybe he'd gone off some crazy deep end, getting into Scientology, or meth, or *Call of Duty*. Would I even *want* to spend time with him?

I guess this was what this lunch was all about: to find out if we were just Facebook friends; if we were lunch-twice-a-year friends; or if we were—maybe, just maybe—actual friend-friends.

But in order to meet him, I had to get to the restaurant. Otto lived in Fairfax, so we agreed to meet at a place halfway between us: Big Mama's and Papa's Pizzeria on Sunset.

Stupidly, I drove. I'd been in Los Angeles less than a week, so I still wasn't used to the traffic—or, more specifically, the asshole drivers. People tailgated, ran lights, cut me off, didn't let me merge, texted and talked on their phones, and—of course—honked at me or flipped me off, like whatever asshole thing *they'd* just done was somehow *my* fault.

I'm sure it has something to do with all those people being crammed into one city, but it somehow turns drivers into sociopaths. And here I was, tooling around in our little Mazda, totally unprepared for all this, like a fragile fawn on its wobbly legs about to be attacked by a snarling grizzly.

Meanwhile, the day was stinking hot. Even in early

September, Los Angeles had this scorching heat, so hot it almost stung, like the sharp jab of a needle at the doctor's office. I wasn't used to this either.

Remember how the night before I'd been all, *Wow, isn't it magical, being in the river of Hollywood history, surrounded by all those hot gay ghosts?* By the time I got to the restaurant and found parking, those feelings were almost entirely gone.

The pizzeria was a hole in the wall, more take-out than actual sit-down, though they had a few tables. Otto was sitting at one of them, lost in his smartphone.

He looked different from the last time I'd seen him, three years earlier. He was a bit thicker, more of a man, but still lean. He was better-dressed than I expected: casual yet somehow expensive. Basically, he looked like almost every other twentysomething guy in this town.

Except for his face.

Otto is a burn-survivor. When he was seven years old, he got into some gasoline with some matches, and it left a scar on his shoulder, neck, and half his face (and also the top of his head where he wears a hair weave, but you'd never in a million years know it). The scar itself is sort of a vague swirl pattern, the gathering of a hurricane, and the eye of the storm is his actual eye.

I'm probably making his scars sound more shocking than they are. If you met him, you'd notice them, and it would probably be the first thing you'd notice. But Otto's face had changed as he'd grown up—the scar had healed more, I guess—and I knew he'd had more plastic surgery too. So now while you'd never not notice the scar, it's not like he's the Elephant Man (not that it would make him a bad person if he was). Basically, he looks no worse than the villain in a James Bond movie.

When Otto and I had been boyfriends, the scar had eventually become sort of invisible to me. He'd just been "Otto," you know? I was sort of embarrassed that I was noticing it again, even if it was actually less obvious than at any time I'd ever known him.

I was worried he'd catch me staring, so I hurried forward and said, "Otto! Sorry I'm late."

He looked up. "Russel! Whoa, I can't believe it. You're really here! It's, like, cognitive dissonance."

There was an instant of hesitation, but then he stood up and we hugged. He smelled good, also like every other guy in Los Angeles. But the hug was nice.

"I know," I said, pulling away and sitting. "I can't believe it either. I actually live here! I'm still not used to the heat. Towels that actually dry out between showers, what a concept? But the traffic...that's why I'm late."

"Yeah, you'll end up planning your whole day around the traffic. And wherever you are, the place you need to be is always two hours away."

We didn't say anything for a second. Then I noticed a photo on the wall.

"Oh, hey!" I said, pointing. "Did you know this was the place that Ellen ordered pizza from during the Oscars two years ago? You know, when she took that selfie with Brad Pitt and Julia Roberts?"

"Yeah," Otto said. "Sorry about that. But the pizza's really good."

*Why are you sorry?* I wanted to say. *I think it's great!* Then I realized that things that seemed new and different to me—the Walk of Fame! The place where Ellen ordered pizza for the Oscars!—were probably hackneyed and tourist-y to someone who lived in Los Angeles, someone like Otto.

"How's Kevin?" Otto asked, and this was awkward too. I'd dated Kevin before Otto, and then Kevin and I had ended up together, so my relationship was sort of weird to talk about with Otto.

"He's fine," I said. "We're good."

"I'm glad."

"What about you? Are you seeing anyone?"

He shook it off. "Nah."

I wasn't sure whether to ask for more details, but I also didn't want to just change the subject. Wasn't that sort of patronizing?

"Maybe we should order?" I said, and Otto nodded.

Up at the counter, we both ordered slices.

"You just want one," Otto said. "Trust me, they're *massive*."

As Otto gave the guy his order, I glanced over at him. I was seeing his good side now—er, his non-scarred side—so I noticed his eyes. I'd forgotten how striking they were, how they were this sort of dark burgundy color, brown with a hint of crimson. Meanwhile, his hair was the color of honey—lighter than before, either bleached by the sun, or maybe he lightened it. He had a great haircut too, a casual tousle, not perfectly gelled.

He was right about the slices. They were almost the size of traffic cones.

Back at the table, I said, "Do you like the people? Here in L.A.? Because the rumor is that they're full of themselves."

He laughed. "Oh, yeah, they totally are! Which is kind of ironic, because I swear to God, every single person who moves to Los Angeles was a total dork in high school. Then they start working out, and get their teeth done, and suddenly they're the beautiful people that their ex-tormentors back in their home town will spend the rest of their lives lusting after and trying to imitate. It's really funny when you think about it. But yeah, even though everyone here is a former dork and should totally know better, they're all judge-y too, just like in high school. Maybe even worse. Nothing ever changes."

"Yeah," I said, but it suddenly felt strange talking about beautiful people with Otto, so I didn't know what to say. I couldn't help but wonder: in an industry full of beautiful people, where did a guy like him fit in? I wanted to ask him, but his scars weren't something we'd talked about in a long, long time. That made me think: Okay, maybe we're really not friends anymore. But that didn't mean we couldn't be again, right?

I put my slice down (it was good, but greasy).

"This feels weird," I said. "Our seeing each other? It's just been so long. You know?"

This was a risky strategy, calling attention to the awkwardness. I'd learned long ago, like on first dates or whatever, that pointing out when something feels awkward can be a good thing, at least if the other person agrees with you. Then they laugh and smile, and you both joke about the awkwardness. It creates this moment of connection that sort of reboots the conversation, diffusing the awkwardness. On the other hand, if the other person doesn't respond, if they just stare at you like you're an idiot for bringing it up, that can actually make the awkwardness even worse.

Otto laughed. "I know!" he said. "And we're not just friends who haven't seen each other in four years, we're *ex-boyfriends*. Talk about pressure. I'm actually pitting through my shirt right now."

"Oh, God, because of me? Please. Stop that sweating this instant! Speaking of which, how does everyone smell so good in this town? I'm sweating because it's so hot, so I feel like I stink."

"Gold Bond Ultimate Comfort."

I just stared at him, even as I picked up my pizza again.

"Body powder?" he said. "Get to know it well. It's totally your new best friend."

"Oh! That actually makes sense. Okay, next question: what about the wardrobe? Everywhere I go, I feel like someone's tag-along little brother. But then I look at what people are wearing, and it doesn't look that different from me. I mean, most people just wear shorts and a shirt. I'm wearing shorts and a shirt, but I feel like I'm doing something wrong. So what am I doing wrong?"

"Your shoes," he said immediately, without even looking me up and down, which was actually sort of revealing. He'd already noticed I was wearing the wrong shoes?

I stuck a foot out. "What about 'em?"

"What are you, a thirteen-year-old girl?"

It's true, they were Onitsuka Tigers, which I'd bought solely because they were on sale (and comfortable).

"Maybe I'm being ironic," I said, my mouth full.

"You're not. Besides, that excuse stopped working three years ago."

I swallowed. "Okay, so I need new shoes."

"Not just that," Otto said. "You need to fully understand the function of shoes in Los Angeles."

"To cover your feet?"

"Not even close. In this town, everyone dresses incredibly casually. That just makes the shoes so much more important. They tell people who you are."

I glanced down at Otto's shoes—some kind of well-worn leather loafer. They looked nice, but I didn't know anything about shoes, so I didn't know how impressed to be.

"You want your shoes to say you're rich and successful," Otto went on, "except you can't be too obvious about it or it'll look fake. It's all part of the Bullshit Factor."

"The what?"

"It's the way this town works. Everyone overstates their accomplishments by a factor of three. So if, say, someone says, 'I have this horror project in development with Guillermo del Toro,' what they really mean is, 'I have a pitch meeting with Eli Roth.' Basically, you take the truth and make it three times more impressive. But you never want to lie outright, or even overdo it. You don't want to say, 'I'm really good friends with Tina Fey,' because that kind of thing always comes back to haunt you."

"And this has what to do with shoes?" I said.

Otto looked slightly exasperated with me. "It's all part of the image you present to the world. That you're incredibly successful and everyone wants to work with you. Just not quite so successful that everyone should have heard of you, so it's obvious you're lying."

"Maybe I'll just go barefoot."

Otto kept glaring at me.

"Okay, okay," I said. "So I need to buy expensive new shoes."

He thought for a second. "Wait a minute, hold the phone. I just realized you fall under the Screenwriter Loophole."

My head was officially spinning. "The what?"

"Well, I said before that everyone in this town is a former dork, which is totally true. But screenwriters are the one group of people in town who don't ever seem to make the leap from 'dork' to 'ex-dork'."

"What do you mean?" I said.

"Most of you stay dorks."

I didn't know very many writers, but this didn't surprise me in the least. "Okay, well, how is that a good thing?"

"It's a good thing because everyone *expects* screenwriters to be dorky and unfashionable. So you show up wearing anything better than a burlap sack, and you're already ahead of the competition. And if you're actually capable of making eye contact, hell, you're halfway to an Oscar right there."

I know I should have been offended, but I couldn't help but smile. "You're making screenwriters sound like total social rejects."

"Oh, I'm sorry, I didn't mean that," Otto said. "I meant *all* writers. You know, TV writers and novelists and playwrights too?"

I cracked up. I loved the irony of this, the guy with the scar on his face instructing the non-scarred guy on how to not be a social pariah. But then I realized I was still obsessing about the scar on Otto's face, and that made me feel guilty.

"It's different for actors," Otto said. "Well, it's not that different. Everyone expects actors to be narcissistic and crazy, which, if I'm totally honest, we basically are. But when it comes to the way we look, that *is* different. We're expected to look a certain way."

In college, Otto had gotten into acting and ended up a theater major—although, depressingly, his biggest role in school really had been the Elephant Man. Once he graduated, he'd set his sights on making it as a TV and movie actor. He'd gotten an agent and had a few roles, mostly in indie movies. But (also very depressingly), he'd played a lot of zombies.

He'd sighed when he'd said that, how actors were supposed to look a certain way.

"How's it going with that?" I said gently. "The acting, I mean."

He sort of shrugged and rolled his eyes. "It's going. Still no SAG card, but I'm not sure that would be a good move for me right now anyway." I knew enough to know that getting a SAG card—becoming a member of the Screen Actors Guild—meant more money per acting job, but it also meant that you couldn't ever do non-union acting jobs, like small indie films, and that was most of the work for actors like Otto.

I looked at him, encouraging him on.

"My agent says we're in a strange time," Otto said. "There's pressure on writers and producers to be more inclusive, to, like, include disabled characters, and not just the usual 'pity' roles, or the teach-the-able-bodied-person-a-lesson roles. But most people still think of 'disability' as a thing that happens *to* you, not an actual identity. You know? They just don't get it."

Otto and I really had fallen out of contact: I hadn't even known that he thought of himself as "disabled." Or had I? I guess he posted links to stuff like this, and I sometimes "liked" them, but I hadn't really read them. But I nodded along. What he was saying made sense.

"Plus, there isn't really a pool of acting talent yet," Otto went on. "So casting directors can legitimately say, 'We couldn't find anyone disabled for the part.' But how could there be a pool of talent? There aren't enough roles for any of us to make a living! But the greater problem is that no one even thinks twice about casting an able-bodied actor in a disabled role. It was one thing when it was Daniel Day-Lewis in *My Left Foot*, or even Kevin McHale on *Glee*. Those were cast a long time ago. But Ansel Elgort in *The Fault in Our Stars*? Eddie Redmayne in *The Theory of Everything*? Come on! My agent says that someday that's going to be looked on like casting a white actor in an Asian role—like they used to do all the time, but they don't anymore. But we're not there yet. So yeah, it's a struggle."

"I'm sorry," I said. "That really sucks."

"Whatever," Otto said. "Acting's a tough life. I knew that going in. It's tough for all actors, not just me. Only in different ways."

"Still." It was breaking my heart to see Otto so down like this.

He shrugged. "Things are changing. My agent says that all the time too. Say what you will about Ryan Murphy, but who else is casting actors with Down

Syndrome? Oh, and look at Miles Teller. He's Mr. Fantastic in *The Fantastic Four.*"

I stared at Otto. Why should I be looking at Miles Teller?

"He has facial scars?" Otto said. "He was in a car accident in 2007. He's got scars all over his face and body."

*He does?* I thought.

"Oh, wow," I said. "Yeah, you're right."

"I know," Otto said. "His scars are a lot less obvious than mine. But they're still visible. My agent says that ten years ago, there's no way he could've had a career as a leading man, no matter how talented he was. But now he's the real deal. We're living in a whole new world where the whole definition of 'beauty' is changing."

"That's great," I said. And even if Otto was maybe being a bit optimistic about how quickly things were changing, I did think what he was saying was great.

"What about you?" Otto asked me. "How's your writing going?"

I was almost done with my pizza by now. I swallowed the last bite, then tried (unsuccessfully) to wipe my greasy fingers clean on a napkin.

"Well, that's kinda the thing," I said. "Everyone said, 'If you want to be a screenwriter, you need to move to Los Angeles.' So Kevin and I moved to Los Angeles. But now what? I'm here, so what do I do? It's not like I can go up to a producer and say, 'Hey, wanna read my screenplay?' I mean, that's what producers always joke about, right? How people are always handing them screenplays at the urinal? So what do I *do*? I'm going to keep sending out my scripts, and agents and producers will probably keep ignoring them, but I could do that when I was back in Seattle. I don't understand how being in Los Angeles helps."

Otto finished the last of his pizza too. "Yeah, it doesn't work like that. It's all about who you know. You have to get to know people. And you will."

"How? No one ever gets out of their cars!"

Otto smiled. "You have to start small. That's what everyone thinks—that you move to Los Angeles, and then someone 'discovers' you, and a few months later, you're a big movie star. But it literally *never* happens that way. Or it happened that way once, back in the 1940s, and people have been talking about it ever since. The way it really works is that you work on some dumb little student film with someone, and then six months later, that director gets a chance to direct an episode of *The Goldbergs*, but you were cool and he's kept following you on Twitter, so he asks you to do a role that only has one line, but then you meet someone on that set, and that leads to something else, and so on and so on. Or maybe some casting director watches that dumb little student film, which probably totally sucks, but sees that you're right for a small part she has, so she calls you in to read, and you don't get that part, but you had a good audition, and you weren't a jerk, so that same casting directing calls you in for another small role three months later, and you actually get that. And then, after three years of stuff like that, you get a part in a pilot that doesn't get picked up, but it leads to a supporting role in a movie, which turns out to be a surprise hit and you're singled out, and then you finally get a leading role, and that's a hit too, and you're singled out again. *That's* how people become movie stars in Hollywood."

"That was a great description of how an actor breaks in," I said. "But how does that help me?"

Otto froze. Then he scrunched up his face. "Oh, my God, you're right. I'm such a typical actor, totally self-absorbed! Russel, I'm sorry. I'm such an asshole."

He had kept grimacing out his apology, overdoing it, and I laughed, but I also couldn't help but notice two things. The first was that he really did have an expressive face, almost elastic. I'd only ever seen Otto act in a couple of short films, and it's hard to tell anything when someone is playing a zombie. But I was starting to think that maybe he was a pretty good actor after all.

The second thing I noticed was how handsome he was. Why hadn't I seen it immediately when I'd walked into the restaurant? I really hadn't been able to see beyond the scars. Now it was back to like it had been before, when we'd been boyfriends, how I didn't see the scar, just *him*, how adorable he was. But it was more than that too. He really had grown into his looks. He was *classically* handsome: firm jaw, straight nose, high cheekbones. He clearly worked out, so much so that just looking at him made me feel tired (and guilty that Kevin and I still hadn't found a new gym). How could I not have noticed all this right away? At least I'd noticed the hair and those amazing eyes. In spite of everything—or maybe just in spite of his scars—I really could see Otto becoming a movie star one day, like Miles Teller.

"It's okay," I said, still laughing, enjoying the moment. Our food was all gone now—our sodas were empty too—but neither one of us made any motion to leave.

Otto got serious again. "I'm not a screenwriter," he said. "But the one thing I do know is that everyone says the system is closed, for both actors *and* screenwriters. That no one can ever break in. Yeah, then, how come so many people *do*? This town loves new talent! It's mostly because they don't have to pay us as much, but hey, whatever. People break through every single day. As for breaking in as a screenwriter, I bet it's the same as with acting. It's like the shoe thing. There are unwritten rules, and you just need to learn them. But you will. They're not that hard. If I can learn the acting rules, you can learn the screen-writing ones."

I nodded, but not very enthusiastically. I admit I was being a baby about the whole screenwriter thing. I mean, I'd only been in Los Angeles for three days, and I'd only been writing screenplays for about a year, and Otto had been acting for six years already (including college). But I still thought it was okay to feel overwhelmed.

"Or!" I said. "Maybe some producer will call me up out of the blue and say, 'I want to produce your movie.'"

Otto's face turned to stone. "Um, what did I just say? That literally *never* happens."

"It *could*."

"How?"

"Well...maybe Steven Spielberg'll get a wrong number, and I'll answer, and before he knows he's talking to the wrong person, I'll have so impressed him with my charm and intellect, he'll have no choice but want to work with me."

"Oh, well, when you put it like *that*."

"Okay, okay, so it's possible I might also need a Plan B," I said.

"Ya think?"

"I need to make some friends in the industry. But I have absolutely no idea how to do that."

"Oh, that's easy in this town. You just need to step outside. And the good news is, you already have one."

"One what?" I said.

"Friend in the industry."

"I do? Who?"

"Me, you idiot!"

I smiled. "Oh. Right." I thought about what I'd been wondering before lunch, about whether Otto and I were still friends. We definitely were. Knowing that, having him in my life, was already making Los Angeles feel a little less overwhelming, a little more like home. Just in terms of him being an actual friend in the industry, it was kind of surreal how much I'd learned from him in one single lunch: the Bullshit Factor, the Screenwriter Loophole, and more.

Even now, neither one of us made a motion to leave.

I fiddled with the hot red peppers. "I've really missed you," I said, not meeting his eyes.

"Me too," he said.

I looked up to him smiling back at me.

"I'd forgotten how much I like you," he said.

We stared at each other for a second, no one saying anything. It was one of those moments of connection I mentioned earlier. At the same time, there wasn't any weird sexual subtext, at least not much of it. We really were friends now—just friends. But good friends.

It was the first time in my life I'd ever rediscovered an old friend, which was great, like taking the cushions off the couch and finding a lost wallet full of money. It was actually better than making a new friend, because there was almost no chance he'd turn out to be moody, or passive-aggressive, or end up fucking my boyfriend. It was like meeting a new person you like, but knowing for a fact you'll actually end up best buddies.

Later that afternoon, Kevin and I went down to the pool again. I'd spent my whole life in damp, rainy Washington State, so I'd always thought of a swimming pool as something sort of fringe-y and extra, like a trampoline. Here in blistering hot Los Angeles, I was starting to think of a pool as something almost essential, like a bed.

"How's Otto?" Kevin asked me, sounding casual, but I knew he had to be at least a little jealous. After all, Otto was still an ex-boyfriend.

"He's actually really good," I said. I told him about Otto's plan to make it big, despite his scars. I couldn't decide if it would be reassuring to tell him there were no longer any sexual feelings (despite how great Otto looked), or if that would come across as defensive, so I didn't say anything.

"How'd the job go?" I said.

Back in Seattle, Kevin had worked as an editor for IMDb (which is actually part of Amazon.com). When he told them we were moving to Los Angeles, they asked him to stay on as a freelance consultant. The plan had been for him to go to events and interview celebrities. It had sounded kind of exciting, plus we needed the steady income, so he'd said yes.

"So far they've got me doing exactly what I was doing back in Seattle," he said.

"For half the pay," I said, and he nodded glumly.

Later, after we'd dried off, we ran into a woman with her teenage son, both Latino, just coming in. She was probably in her thirties, well-dressed, like for an office, but with maybe too much starch. A receptionist, I decided. She looked tired. She didn't have the weight of the whole world on her shoulders, but there was at least a pretty good portion of Southern California.

Her son was seventeen or eighteen, with long cotton pants and a polo shirt, both of them dirty and rumpled. Everything that could be untucked was untucked, including his pockets, which were pulled up out of his pants. (Seriously, was this a "thing"? It had been six years since I'd been in high school, so I didn't know.)

"¡Dios Mio!" he was saying. "¡No mames!"

"Can we please not argue about this?" she was saying to him. "Just this once?"

We met at the bottom of the stairway and did that awkward dance about who was going to go up first. Technically, we'd arrived there about a second before them, but she was older, and a woman, and also carrying a bag of groceries, so Kevin and I shuffled back away from the stairs.

"Hey there," Kevin said. He motioned to the steps. "Go ahead."

She hesitated, like she was trying to decide whether

to thank us, and I said, "I'm Russel, this is Kevin. We just moved in."

"Yeah, I saw." She forced out a smile. "I'm Zoe, and this is my brother Daniel."

So they were siblings, not mother and son. But it sure looked like she was raising him. I wondered what the story was.

"Hey," I said to Daniel.

He didn't answer. Maybe he didn't speak English, but it felt more like he couldn't be bothered responding. There was an air of mischievousness about him, or maybe even outright defiance, like he was one of the trickster gods, Loki in Norse mythology, or Prometheus among the Greeks.

Zoe looked like she'd had it, so before we could say anything else, she said, "Well, it's nice to meet you both." Then she trudged up the stairs.

As they disappeared, I glanced up at Daniel again. He was still ignoring me, but I should probably point out that he was a little like a Greek or Norse god in one other way too: teenager or not, he was one of the cutest guys I'd ever seen.

The following week, after we were *finally* unpacked, Kevin was washing the dishes after dinner, and I was trying to preheat the oven so I could make cookies. But the oven was gas, and so old it didn't even have a pilot light. You had to actually open the oven up and light it with a match.

As I was trying to light it, I said to Kevin, "Maybe this is how he did it. The guy who killed himself in our apartment? He put his head in the gas oven?"

"We don't even know if that's true," Kevin said.

"Yeah, but if it is true, maybe he did it here. It sure looks old enough." It was kind of creepy looking into that darkened oven, thinking that someone might have once died there, in the exact spot where I was now.

The apartment had no dishwasher, so Kevin was drying the dishes by hand. "Who knows?" he said. "I bet it's just a story."

"Yeah," I said.

The oven still wasn't lighting. How the hell hard was it to light natural gas anyway? I'd turned the crank.

Then I realized something. "I don't smell any-thing," I said. "I'm not even sure the gas is turned on. But doesn't it have to be? I mean, doesn't the hot water tank use gas? Darn it, I wanted to make snicker-doodles."

"Make what?" Kevin said.

"They were my favorite cookie as a kid."

"We need to call the landlord."

I sat back on my heels. "Not yet. I should totally be able to figure this out. Especially since I'm the butch one in this relationship."

Kevin rolled his eyes. "Are we really doing this?"

"What?" I said matter-of-factly. "You know it's true. It's what everyone says after they meet us. We're both butch, but I'm the *impossibly* butch one."

"First of all, who cares who's butch? Aren't we beyond all that by now? But if someone *did* care, the fact that you have to *be* the butch one just proves how totally insecure you are, that you're not really the butch one."

Hmmm, Kevin had a good point. I'd expected this

sparring to go on longer. But he'd already teased me into a corner.

"You know," I said, "I think I liked you better back in high school when you were a dumb jock."

Kevin laughed.

In the other room, my phone chimed. I couldn't think the last time someone had actually *called* me.

"It's probably your mom asking if we're okay," Kevin said.

Thinking he was right, I almost ignored it. But I didn't know what else to do to get the stove lit, so I decided to take the call after all.

*Unknown caller*, the screen said.

I answered it. "This is Russel."

"Russel Middlebrook?" said the voice on the other end of the line.

"That's me. Who's this?"

"My name is Lewis Dunn. I'm the personal assistant to Isaac Brander. He's read your screenplay *A Cup of Joe*, and he'd love to talk to you about it."

I was confused. "What?"

"Are you the author of *A Cup of Joe?*" the voice said. "The screenplay?"

"Yeah," I said, still confused. I'd written that screenplay earlier in the year. It was sort of a romantic "dramedy," the story of a twenty-three-year-old barista named Joe living in Seattle, unhappy with his life. He runs into his old boyfriend from high school, Milo, and decides that getting back together with him will solve all his problems, but Milo has a new boyfriend now. Meanwhile, in an interweaving "flashback" storyline, we learn the real story behind Joe and Milo's relationship in high school (which isn't at all what you think).

The screenplay was (very, very loosely) based on my relationship with Kevin, and I'd been pretty happy with it. It was a "gay" story, but it wasn't *about* being gay. There was no gay angst, not even in the high school flashbacks, and there was also no straight female best friend, no bitchy gay sidekick, and absolutely no gay hustlers or self-destructive party boys. It was just the story of two guys trying to figure out their lives.

I'd sent out a bunch of query emails to agents and producers, but only a couple had even responded. I'd also entered a bunch of (expensive) screenwriting contests, placed in a couple, and also put the script on TheBlackList.com and Inktip.com—two (expensive) websites where writers post their scripts so "Hollywood insiders" can supposedly read them. But no one had ever gotten back to me. The problem hadn't been finding people willing to take my money in order to get the word out about my screenplay. The problem had been finding any Hollywood insiders who actually gave a fuck about reading it.

"Didn't you send Mr. Brander your script?" said the voice on the phone.

It was finally becoming clear to me: I was hearing back from one of the handful of people who had actually requested my screenplay.

"Oh!" I said. "Yes! Of course. Let me just check my notes," I said, brazenly lying. I hesitated a moment, checking nothing whatsoever. Then I said, "Yes, I absolutely did send Mr. Brander my script. You just caught me by surprise."

"Well, Mr. Brander would like to talk to you," the voice said.

"About what?"

Yes, I really am that slow.

There was a moment's hesitation on the other end. I, of course, kept kicking myself.

"Um, about your script," the voice said. "Mr. Brander thinks he might be able to do something with it."

*Do something?* I thought. *As in, turn it into a movie?* This couldn't really be happening. Could it?

"Do you have representation?" the voice said.

"Uh, not currently, but I've been talking to a couple of different agents." Translation: one single agent had requested a different screenplay of mine six months ago, and I hadn't heard a damn thing from him ever since.

"You're based here in town, right? The screenplay says you are."

That meant this was a *recent* submission. I'd started putting our new address on my scripts three weeks ago, right after Kevin and I had signed the lease. Someone had told me that producers paid more attention to screenplays with Los Angeles addresses. Apparently they were right!

"I am based in Los Angeles," I said. "Just off Franklin and Ivar. I was just out in the pool!"

Okay, so that was probably too much detail. But he ignored it.

"Would you be willing to come for a meeting with Mr. Brander?"

"Let me just check my calendar," I said, brazenly lying again. "Yes, I think I might possibly be able to make that happen." It was only after I said this that I realized he hadn't given me a time or a date yet. So much for the Bullshit Factor.

"Tomorrow at one?"

I thought about "consulting my calendar" again, but that seemed sort of ridiculous at this point.

"Tomorrow at one would be perfect."

"Would you be willing to meet here at the house? It's quite a bit more convenient for Mr. Brander."

"No, sure, that's fine." Then I listened while he gave me the address. He only had to repeat it four times as I scrambled for a pen and paper, and then (of course) the pen didn't work at first.

Finally, I had the address, and I hung up the phone. I found Kevin in the kitchen. "You're not going to believe who that was."

"Who was it?"

I told him.

He stared at me, confused. He didn't understand. I hadn't understood at first either. I wasn't sure I understood now.

"You're kidding, right?" he said.

"I'm not kidding. That's who was just on the phone." Kevin already knew how I'd been submitting scripts for months now.

"This has to be a scam or something," Kevin said.

"Yeah," I said. Even now, I was "excited," but not *excited*, because this couldn't possibly be real. My sixth day in Hollywood and a producer calls me up and wants to produce one of my scripts? What were the odds?

"We need to look him up," Kevin said.

"Huh?" I said.

"On IMDb." The full name of the company Kevin worked for was the Internet Movie Database, and it happens to be the definitive list of everyone who's anyone in Hollywood. "What was his name again?"

I looked at the piece of paper. Of course I hadn't

written it down—I'd only written the address. I hadn't written the assistant's name either.

"Emmett Brander," I said. "No, wait, Isaac, I think."

Kevin was already sitting down at the computer. He typed and scanned for a minute.

"Well?" I said.

He sat back in the chair. He was either totally disgusted or dutifully impressed, and I couldn't tell which.

"What?" I said. "*What?*"

"If this is the guy he says he is, he's made movies with Sally Field. And Robert Redford. And Burt Reynolds."

I read the list of his credits. It was a whole bunch of movies I recognized, and a few I'd actually seen. Kevin and I stared at each other now.

*There has to be a catch,* I thought.

Otto and I had joked about a producer calling me up and wanting to produce my screenplays. He'd said that didn't happen—that people didn't just breeze into town and become superstars. Otto had specifically said that it had happened, like, once in the whole history of the city.

But maybe it had finally happened a second time. And maybe the person it had finally happened to was me.

# CHAPTER THREE

Needless to say, I barely slept all night. How would the meeting go? What would I say? More importantly, what would I *wear*? I knew what *I* thought looked good, but as Otto had made vividly clear, I had completely failed the Los Angeles "shoe" test. I owned a grand total of three pairs of shoes, one of which were my Onitsuka Tigers, and the other was a pair of Ecco dress shoes, like for a jacket and tie. Sadly, Kevin and I wore different shoe sizes. So I had to rely on my one pair of generic "dress casual" shoes, and hope that Mr. Brander knew about the Screenwriter Loophole, at least until Otto could take me out shopping. The good news is I'd picked up some Gold Bond at CVS the night before.

I planned on arriving at the meeting forty-five minutes early in case anything went wrong.

Something did go wrong: I got stuck in traffic. I was also nearly killed when a minivan almost sideswiped me on North Cahuenga, but I was rapidly discovering that kind of thing was so commonplace that it was barely even worth mentioning. I could actually see Kevin and me in three months, with me coming home to our apartment after another meeting:

Kevin: Oh, hey, anything unusual happen today?
Me: I almost got killed three times on my way to Burbank.
Kevin: So nothing unusual?

Then, of course, I got lost. The house was off Sunset Boulevard, in a hilly neighborhood just before Silver Lake. Some of the houses looked pretty nice, others not so much: a perfectly tended garden of succulents and crushed granite gravel on one side of the street, a chain-link fence and concrete cinder-blocks on the other. This was clearly an area in transition, but I couldn't quite tell if it was transition-ing up or down.

Finally, I found the address with a whole six minutes to spare. Was it a good idea to be fashionably late to something like this? I thought about texting to ask Otto, but decided I didn't even want to try to be That Guy, especially since I already knew I didn't have the right shoes, and I couldn't really be That Guy under the best of circumstances.

I parked along the street, but the house itself was hidden behind a huge, untrimmed hedge. I walked along looking for an entrance, but there was no way in except the gated driveway, which had a little intercom on a metal pole positioned to one side. That made me think I'd already made a blunder, that I was supposed to drive up into the driveway in my car, not walk in. But I was already on the verge of being late, and I was absolutely positive that I didn't want Isaac

Brander to see my car anyway. My car was even more embarrassing than my shoes!

I walked to the intercom and was about to press the button when I had to stop and take a moment. This was it: the place and time where my screen-writing career could very well make a massive leap forward. Conversely, I could say or do something stupid, and the whole thing would disappear around me.

"Russel?" said the voice on the intercom, even before I'd pushed anything.

Of course I jumped.

"Yeah?" I said, but I wasn't sure to whom. Did I need to press a button to talk? I noticed a little camera on the intercom. So they could see me, but I couldn't see them. That figured.

The intercom buzzed, and the gate slowly swung open. I stepped into the yard.

Like the neighborhood around it, the yard was in transition too, but this time I had a clear idea which direction it was going: down. The landscaping had probably been really impressive in its day, but some-one must have laid off the gardener. It was one of those yards where everything looks overgrown and dying at exactly the same time. Nothing had been trimmed, and the grass was long dead. Then again, California was in the middle of this terrible drought, so pretty much all the grass in the city was dead.

The residence—somehow more than a house, but less than a mansion—was old too, maybe even from the 1940s. It was some kind of tan adobe with a red terracotta roof. I'm not entirely sure what Spanish Colonial is, but let's say it was that. It could've used a coat of paint, but it's not like it was the setting to some dystopian YA novel.

The front door was already open when I got there, so I stepped inside. It was dark and cool, but not the unnatural cool of air conditioning. Did it have something to do with the architecture? Or maybe it was just the contrast with the mid-day sun.

My eyes adjusted. The floor was red tile, polished so it reflected, and the walls were dark wood paneling with lots of whirls and knots. Antique furnishings materialized around me—a bureau by the door, tables and chairs in the room beyond. On one shelf, I saw a set of three differently-sized elephants carved out of jade. The house smelled like something rich and exotic. I'm also not quite sure what patchouli smells like, but let's say it smelled like that. And there was something medicine-y, like menthol.

"Russel," a voice said.

"That's me," I said, turning. I'd been determined not to jump again, and I hadn't.

It was a black guy, good-looking, clean-cut, early thirties maybe, well-dressed in slacks and a button-down shirt—nice, but not that nice. He had good posture and even better eye contact.

"I'm Lewis, Mr. Brander's personal assistant," the guy said. "We spoke on the phone?"

"Right! Hi, there." I shook his hand. At the same time, I couldn't resist glancing down at his shoes. But since I didn't know anything about shoes, that didn't really tell me anything. Or maybe it did: they could've used a bit of polish, which made me feel better. I also tried to smell him, to see if he wore cologne, or even Gold Bond Ultimate Comfort, but I couldn't smell anything at all.

"Mr. Brander is waiting for you in his office," Lewis said.

I followed him deeper into the house. I caught the lingering scent of bleach, as if someone had cleaned recently. Being here felt a little like I was going back in time again, to the days of Humphrey Bogart and Lauren Bacall, or maybe just a video I'd once seen for that old Eagles song "Hotel California."

My footsteps echoed on the tile, but somehow Lewis' didn't (softer soles?). I knew I should still be nervous, and I was, but not like I expected. Maybe it was the fact that this was so wildly out of my experience. It wasn't like going on a first date, or pining for some hot guy in French class. So I didn't really know *how* to react. Or maybe my emotions hadn't caught up with me yet—they were lagging behind me, wandering around like a wide-eyed puppy finally off its leash.

Lewis led me into Mr. Brander's home office. There was a big picture window opposite the doorway and the sun was shining in, and after the darkness of the hallway, my eyes had to adjust again.

The first thing I noticed were the framed movie posters on the walls, of all the movies I'd seen on IMDb the night before. In between the posters, there were framed pictures of people: mostly men, mostly young, mostly very attractive. There were shelves too, built-ins, with mementos on them. I saw awards—I spotted a Golden Globe, and an Emmy, but no Oscars—and weird things like an antique hookah, a stuffed owl, and a packet of old Melachrino cigarettes encased in acrylic. It was probably all stuff that had a story behind it.

A room full of memories.

The sunlight from the window caught dust particles hanging in the air.

On the other side of those particles, a man sat at an old wooden desk.

"Mr. Brander?" Lewis said, and the man turned, and I finally made out his face.

What a face! It should have been staring back at me from Mount Rushmore: old and chiseled and distinguished, and also somehow out of time. It wasn't just that he was old—though he *was* old, in his eighties at least, with thick white hair. It was that he seemed like someone from a truly different era, like how the faces of actors from the 1950s really do seem different from the faces of actors now. Mr. Brander was handsome, or at least had *been* handsome, but it was an exaggeration of a face.

He rolled back away from the desk. It was only then that I realized he was in a wheelchair. (If his face was old-fashioned, his wheelchair was state-of-the-art: sleek and small and expensive.)

"Russel," he said. He hadn't shouted, but his rumble of a voice filled the room as if from speakers. "Thank you so much for coming."

"It's very nice to meet you," I said, stepping forward and offering him my hand.

We shook, and that's when I noticed that unlike Lewis, Mr. Brander had a smell, or at least a hint of one. Unfortunately, it was pee. I looked down to check out his shoes too, but he wasn't wearing any, only leather slippers tucked into the footrests of the wheelchair. They were nice slippers at least.

None of this made any sense. Mr. Brander was a real producer with a long list of impressive credits.

He'd won a Golden Globe, for God's sake. He'd invited me to his house to talk about producing my screenplay, and it had clearly once been a pretty nice place. His personal assistant had good posture and even better eye contact. But the man himself was older than the pyramids, in a wheelchair, and smelled like pee. It was such a weird mix of contradictions.

Or maybe there weren't any real contradictions. Maybe Mr. Brander was just a has-been. I looked back at the posters on the walls of his office. Sally Field. Robert Redford. Burt Reynolds. These were *old* actors. The movies Mr. Brander produced had been back in the 1970s (or earlier). Why hadn't that occurred to me the night before when Kevin and I had looked him up on IMDb? It probably explained the neighborhood too. Back when he bought the place, it had probably been really nice, but that was so long ago the whole area had had time to take a downturn and was now even starting to get nice again.

I was such an idiot. Did I really think becoming a screenwriter would be this easy? Even in movies about Hollywood, where things probably aren't anything like real life, it's never *this* easy for screenwriters to break in. There's always at least a "hard at work" montage.

"Oh, dear," Mr. Brander said. "I've horrified you." His voice was deep, but gentle, soothing. "You didn't expect me to be so old. Or in this chair."

"What?" I said. "No! Not at all." I almost said, "I have a really good friend who has facial scarring, and he's disabled too," but I think that would've made things even more awkward.

"Then there's this old house," Mr. Brander went on. "I swear, all I need is a crazy sister, and suddenly it's *Whatever Happened to Baby Jane?*"

I smiled.

"You know *Whatever Happened to Baby Jane?*" he said.

"Of course," I said. I almost said, "Doesn't everyone?" Then I remembered that the movie was mostly a "gay" thing—campy.

Mr. Brander was gay, of course. I'd known that from the dark wood and antiques in the other rooms—the masculinity of the house—and also the good-looking, smiling men in the photos on the walls and shelves. Then there was the fact that he was interested in my screenplay in the first place. This wasn't really a realization: I'd sort of assumed it all along.

"I worked with Bette Davis," Mr. Brander said, nodding to the star of *Whatever Happened to Baby Jane?* on a poster on the wall (for a movie I'd never heard of). "I've worked with a lot of movie stars, and they all have charisma, but Bette was different. She wasn't beautiful exactly, but you couldn't *not* look at her. More than Marilyn, more than Marlene. She was a walking train wreck, always about to crash. You couldn't look away."

"That's funny," I said, but I didn't laugh.

"Please sit down," Mr. Brander said, nodding to a chair opposite him. "Can we get you something to drink? Coffee? Tea?" I looked over at Lewis, who I hadn't realized was still standing in the doorway.

"Uh, a glass of ice water?" I said. By this point, his perfect posture was kind of annoying me.

"Sure thing," Lewis said, and then he withdrew.

When he was gone, Mr. Brander picked up a small stuffed monkey from the windowsill. It was one of the wind-up kind with the cymbals and the red fez cap, but he didn't wind it up.

Finally, he set it down and looked at me again. "Russel, let me be completely honest with you. I'm old. That's obvious, isn't it?" He laughed, so I smiled. "I haven't produced a movie in more than twenty years. But I produced a lot of movies back in the day. Some of them were quite successful, and one or two of them were even pretty good!" Now I laughed too. "But I never produced the movie I truly *wanted* to produce. I feel like I never made the mark I wanted to make. Now I'm old, but I'm not dead yet. I know how to produce movies. And the one movie I want to produce before I die is *A Cup of Joe*."

Mr. Brander's voice was hypnotic, seductive almost, massaging me with its timbre. I didn't know how to react. Maybe this crazy old man might still be able to produce my screenplay after all. Clint Eastwood was still making movies at age eighty-whatever. On the other hand, Clint Eastwood didn't smell like pee (presumably).

"You're an excellent writer," Mr. Brander said. He nodded to my screenplay, which I hadn't noticed on his desk before. It was dog-eared, and the cover was all marked up. There's a rumor about Hollywood that producers never actually read screenplays: they have their "readers" read screenplays *for* them, and then those readers write up "coverage," which is like a synopsis and which also gives the screenplay's supposed strengths and weaknesses. Mr. Brander may have been older than the Grand Canyon, but at least he'd actually read my screenplay himself.

"There's a freshness to this script that I haven't seen before," he went on. "Whether I make it or someone else does, it's going to make a very fine movie."

"Thanks," I said, blushing. This was literally the first time anyone who wasn't a friend had said anything like that about my writing. Now I knew what people meant when they said, "Flattery will get you everywhere." At that point, I would have washed all the windows in his house if he'd asked.

But what did it matter if he liked my script? He was a smelly old man in a wheelchair, locked away in a dusty old house. He couldn't actually get it made. Could he?

"You're not sure about me," Mr. Brander said, and I was impressed by his ability to know what I was thinking (and a little worried he'd also know I was thinking about how he smelled). "That's okay, I wouldn't be either. But at least let me make my case."

I nodded. Right then, Lewis returned with my water—actually a small bottle of Evian with a glass of ice (and a cup of tea for Mr. Brander). He left again, but I had a feeling that he was lingering somewhere just outside.

"When I was active in Hollywood, there were people who wanted to make movies about gay people. A few of them even did. Did you ever see a film called *Making Love*?"

I shook my head no.

"It doesn't matter," he said. "These people, many of whom were my friends, moved heaven and earth to get those movies made. Most of them didn't suc-ceed. But even the few who did, they faced a furious reaction from the public, the world at large. Movies about gay people used to be a very, very hard sell. Somehow I sensed that. There was a time when I had power in this town, when I had clout. I could have helped those struggling filmmakers. But I didn't. I was afraid. I was a coward. I had my own career to worry about. But those people who made all those brave, daring movies that ended up hurting their careers? They paved the way for the movies we see today—for the *changes* we see today. Do you understand what I'm saying?"

"You want to make amends," I said. "You want to make a gay movie."

"Not just any gay movie. I want to make *your* gay movie. Do you know why?"

I shook my head no again.

"We're finally at a moment in time when movies can tell the truth about gay people." He thought for a second. "It's not that those earlier movies didn't tell the truth. They did. But they were so constrained by the times, and they had to be so many different things to so many different people, that most of them ended up as movies *of* their time. Even *Brokeback Mountain*. It was important to show the mainstream world the reality of gay pain and suffering. But things are different now, and I think we're all tired of doom-and-gloom anyway. The point is, those movies were important, and they always will be, but they're not timeless. But your script? I think it's one for the ages."

At this point, Mr. Brander wasn't just massaging me with his voice. Now it felt more like he was romancing me, like he was leading me in a dance, something mysterious and old-fashioned—a tango. Sure, he was in a wheelchair, and older than primordial ooze, but it almost felt like he was holding me, leading me around the room in his arms, through those motes of dust sparkling in the sunlight from the window, and I was more than willing to follow, step by step, somehow in perfect sync.

"Filmmakers are finally able to tell the truth about our lives," Mr. Brander said. "But so far, I think they're missing something essential. They think being truthful about gay people is showing blowjobs, sex. But hasn't everyone already seen that online? Or they show how horrible gay people can be too, how petty we can be to each other. And that's okay. That's a certain kind of truth, and God knows, gay people have been one-dimensional on film for far too long. But those movies, those TV shows, they don't speak to me, not at my age anyway. Maybe I'm too old, maybe I really am irrelevant, but I think the truly shocking, the truly subversive thing right now would be to make a movie that shows the truth about gay love. Not how neurotic and self-destructive it is, but how strong it is, or at least how strong it can be. And not cheap sentiment—not a romantic fantasy either, but something real and powerful. I think that's what your screenplay shows better than anything I've ever read. Oh, and the high school flashbacks? I absolutely love that it isn't at all what we expect."

The music of Mr. Brander's voice continued to lead me on, whirling me around with his intoxicating words. He really *had* read my script, because he had described *exactly* what I'd been going for. It was something I'd talked a lot about with my mentor Vernie Rose back in Seattle. But honestly? I wasn't entirely sure I'd pulled it off. I mean, it was only the fourth screenplay I'd ever written.

"Before I die," Mr. Brander said, "this is the movie

I want to make. This is the mark I want to leave on the world. This is the truth I want to tell."

The music in my mind, the rhythm of Mr. Brander's voice, came to a dramatic stop, but the feeling of complete and utter devotion I felt for him now went on. Did he want one of my kidneys? He could have it. Hell, he could take 'em both! If he wanted it, I'd throw in my pancreas too.

In the silence that followed, Mr. Brander glanced down to the windowsill again, to one particular photo of a handsome man. I looked around the room and realized that the same man was in a lot of the pictures on the walls—maybe even most of them. Mr. Brander, much younger, was almost always next to him, laughing or arm-in-arm. Right near me was a photo of the two of them on the beach: shirtless, smiling, happy.

*It's his dead partner*, I thought. *That's the truth he wants to tell, the story of his own love.*

It was impossible not to be touched by this. Because my screenplay had been based on my own love for Kevin, I also couldn't help feeling weirdly close to Mr. Brander.

But slowly, little by little, my feet returned to the ground. The sunlight from the window had dimmed, the sparkling motes disappearing around me. This house? Mr. Brander's age? This guy couldn't possibly produce my screenplay, no matter how much I identified with it. On the other hand, as old as he was, he *had* produced movies before, and he'd worked with lots of important people. He still had to have at least a few good contacts. And let's face it, it's not like anyone else was knocking on my door to get my script.

"Lewis tells me you're deciding between a couple of different agents," Mr. Brander said.

I wasn't sure what to say to that. Should I tell him the truth? Finally, I nodded. A lie seems like less of a lie if you don't actually say it out loud.

"When do you think you'll be making a decision?" he said.

"Uh, soon," I said vaguely. It occurred to me: I could call Otto and ask if his agent would represent me. I think Otto had said she represented screenwriters, and I figured she'd be happy to rep a deal that was basically already in place. "Very soon."

"I can't get involved in any kind of bidding war," Mr. Brander said. "We'll need investors, of course, and we'll get them. By all means. But to get them, I need to show them I'm not profligate, that they can trust me with their money. Obviously, I really want to do it, but all I have to offer is my passion for the project."

I was about to say, "It's okay, I wasn't expecting any money upfront," when Mr. Brander went on to say, "But I can offer ten thousand for a one-year option period, with an option for renewal at the same price, against two percent of the budget, a two hundred ceiling, and four points net."

I didn't know for sure what any of that meant, but I was pretty sure that "ten thousand" meant "ten thousand dollars." Which was pretty fucking fantastic, considering I'd been about to agree to "nothing." Even if the movie never got made—and, let's face it, it probably wouldn't—ten thousand dollars was some real money. It also meant I wouldn't have to get a job, at least for a while.

"This isn't going to be a lavish production," Mr.

Brander said. "I'm thinking a budget of around six million. But the script is solid, and I know we can attract some top talent. Once the contracts are signed, I'll want to get started right away. I still have a very good relationship with Sally Field. What do you think of her for the grandmother?"

I couldn't breathe, that's what I thought of Sally Field for the grandmother.

"And who do you see as Joe and Milo?" he asked me.

"I was thinking it might be interesting to go multi-racial for at least one the roles," I said. "Someone like Jussie Smollett."

Mr. Brander looked at me blankly.

"He's on a show called *Empire*," I said. "He's also out, but he plays a gay character on *Empire*, so he might not want to do another one." I thought about what Otto had said about his not being able to even read for roles of characters without scars. "I know another guy who'd be perfect too—a really great actor."

"Excellent, excellent, my boy. Casting is the fun part, you know. It's the one part of movie-making where you don't have to make any compromises. In the end, we're going to have exactly the cast we want."

I nodded as if I had some clue what he was talking about.

"But there'll be lots of time to discuss all this in the months ahead," he said. Then he wheeled himself forward a couple of inches, and I realized this was the wheelchair equivalent of a person standing up. In other words, our meeting was over. "Please have your agent call me as soon as possible."

"Absolutely," I stood up. "And it was really nice to meet you. I'm really flattered—the things you said about my screenplay. That's exactly what I was going for."

He smiled a grin as grateful and as good-looking as the ones in any of the photos on the walls.

As I was turning for the door, I came face to face with one particular photo. It was Mr. Brander, *much* younger—like in his twenties—but not with the handsome man this time. It was someone else, someone I recognized.

"Is that Tennessee Williams?" I said. "The playwright?"

"Hmm?" Mr. Brander said. "Oh. Yes."

"You knew him?"

Mr. Brander smiled broadly. His teeth were yellow, but it was his first truly relaxed smile since I'd met him. Could it be that he'd been as nervous about this meeting as I was—that he'd been thinking he might not get the rights to my screenplay?

"*Know* him?" Mr. Brander said. "I produced the original Broadway production of *Sweet Bird of Youth*. It was my first big production."

I turned to look at him—down at him. "Seriously?"

"Yes," he said. "Oh, I spent many a weekend with him and his partner Frank. Why?"

"It's just that Tennessee Williams is my favorite playwright. He's my favorite *writer*. *The Glass Menagerie* is my favorite play of all time." Worried that I might have offended him, I added, "I like *Sweet Bird of Youth* a lot too."

Mr. Brander smiled, lost in reverie. "'I have tricks in my pocket, I have things up my sleeve,'" he said, quoting from the play. "'But I am the opposite of a stage magician. He gives you illusion that has the appearance of truth. I give you truth in the pleasant disguise of illusion.' You know, Tennessee actually worked at a shoe store when he was younger—not a shoe factory, but close. Just between you and me, I think *Menagerie* is his best play too."

This was all a sign. It had to be, right? Mr. Brander's first big production had been a play by my favorite writer. And his last one was going to be a screenplay by me. What could be more perfect? Yes, Mr. Brander's was a house of contradictions. But they weren't senseless contradictions. They all added up to a perfectly plausible story: Mr. Brander felt the need to redeem himself, and he wanted to do it with my screenplay.

Even better, he wasn't asking me to give up my soul in exchange for success, or anything like that.

I didn't want to get ahead of myself. Maybe this project wouldn't go anywhere. I knew the whole deal could fall through tomorrow. It's not like I was now going to go out looking for just the right spot on that sidewalk on Hollywood Avenue for my own star on the Walk of Fame.

Okay, that was a lie. I *was* getting ahead of myself—way ahead—and I'd probably go out scoping spots for my star on the Walk of Fame too.

But for the time being, I was at least smart enough not to tell that to anyone else.

# CHAPTER FOUR

I've never been a fan of non-linear storytelling. Yes, there are times when it works, when it's important to the theme of a movie, like in *Memento*. In *A Cup of Joe*, I use parallel, interweaving storylines in two different timelines, but they're both linear, and I tried hard to make it all clean and clear. That's because I believe that, first and foremost, it's the job of the writer to just tell the damn story, and not get bogged down with distracting gimmicks or your own self-indulgent artistic pretensions.

Which is why it was so funny when I called Kevin right after the meeting, I couldn't seem to tell him the story of what happened with Mr. Brander in chronological order. I kept jumping around all over the place.

"He worked with Tennessee Williams!" I said into my phone. "He was one of the producers on the original Broadway production of *Sweet Bird of Youth*! He thinks my screenplay is exactly what the world needs right now—that for too long, everything was all doom-and-gloom, but that now everything is either 'shocking' sex or asshole characters, either that or sometimes just romantic fantasy, and that no one is doing what I'm doing—telling the truth about gay love. His house isn't very nice though, the neighbors have a crushed granite gravel garden. Oh, and he's in a wheelchair, and I think he's making this movie because of his handsome dead partner."

When I got back to the apartment, I wasn't much clearer. I guess I was too flustered by everything that had happened.

But in the end, Kevin managed to coax the whole story out of me, from start to finish. For some reason, I never did tell him that Mr. Brander smelled a little bit like pee, I guess because it was so disgusting.

When I was done, Kevin looked at me, thinking, but I couldn't tell what. Was he excited? Skeptical? Still totally confused because, in spite of his efforts to reign me in, my recounting of the story really had been all over the place?

"Well?" I said, seeking clarification.

"You need an agent," he said.

"That's exactly what I thought!" I said. "I was thinking I could call Otto, and he could recommend me to his."

Kevin nodded.

"But what do you *think*?" I said.

He didn't answer for a second, his face still a kaleidoscope of conflicting emotions. Which, to tell the truth, sort of pissed me off. I really, really wanted this thing with Mr. Brander to be real, so I wanted Kevin to validate my hopes that it *was* real—that it had finally "happened" for me, and my screenwriting career now had nowhere to go but up, up, and up!

Kevin isn't like that. He isn't a "Dream it and it will come true!" kind of guy. Which I usually appreciate, because I mostly think those people are insufferable. Either Mr. Brander was the real deal, or he wasn't, and all my dreaming and hoping wasn't going to change that one way or the other. In fact, playing things a bit more cautious now was one way to keep me from having the rug totally yanked out from under me in the end.

But still. The longer Kevin didn't say anything, the more the air was leaking out of me. If I'd been one of those inflatable Santas, or Baymax in *Big Hero 6*, I already would've been tipping over.

"I'll call Otto," I said, pulling my phone out.

"Russel?" he said, stopping me.

I looked at him.

"No matter what happens, this is exciting," he said. "And he's right about your screenplay. It's exactly what the world needs right now."

Then he leaned in and kissed me—not a passionate, let's-pop-the-champagne kiss, but an I-love-you-no-matter-what-happens one.

*Hey, I'll take it,* I thought.

Of course Otto was thrilled for me. (Truthfully, he was a lot more excited than Kevin, but then Otto didn't have to live with me if the deal fell through.) He was also happy to recommend me to his agent, and the next morning, I got a call.

"Hold for Fiona Lang," said the voice on my phone.

"Okay," I said. I knew that was the name of Otto's agent.

A few seconds later, a voice said, "Russel? Fiona Lang."

"Thanks for getting back to me," I said. "Otto says good things about you."

"So tell me about this deal."

I did. I told pretty much the whole story, more coherent than I'd been with Kevin, although once again I made a point to leave out the part about how Mr. Brander smelled.

When I was done, she didn't say anything. Finally, she said, "Jesus, Isaac Brander? He must be older than Moses by now."

"He's not *that* old," I said.

"As far as I can tell, he doesn't even have an office anymore."

"He's working out of his home."

"But why? Isaac Brander hasn't made a film in years."

"Well," I said, "he told me it was because he loved the script."

That shut her up, for a second anyway. The truth is, she sounded put out by this whole conversation, like she was doing me this *huge* favor just talking to me on the phone, which I guess she sort of was.

"Otto tells me you need representation fast," she said. "As a favor to him, I'll agree to handle this deal on a one-time basis. But I'm not necessarily taking you on as a client, is that understood? Not until I get a chance to read your work."

Frankly, I was finding this all a little surreal. She was an agent, right? This was what she did: represent deals like this. So here I was, a writer coming to her with *an offer already in place* from a famous movie producer, but she was giving me all this attitude. I kind of wanted to tell her to go fuck herself.

But she was also Otto's agent, and he'd stuck his

neck out for me, and I didn't want to get him in trouble. Plus, the fact was I *did* need an agent fast, and I had this weird feeling that almost any agent I talked to would react about the same way.

"Understood," I said. "I'll send you his contact info, and a couple of my screenplays, as soon as we get off the phone."

She grunted and hung up before I could even ask for her email address (but I knew I could get it from Otto).

Would Fiona Lang have given more of a flying fuck about me if the offer on my screenplay had come from Christopher Nolan, or if it really had been Steven Spielberg who'd called me up? Probably. But that just confirmed something I'd already suspected about agents and managers: they're totally willing to help out new talent, but not until you reach the point where you've pretty much made it, and you don't need their help anymore.

So now came the waiting. How long did it take to negotiate a movie contract anyway? I had no idea, and I didn't want to bother Otto again. Kevin was out on an interview, so I spent the next couple of hours pacing back and forth in the apartment, waiting for Fiona to call back. I couldn't help but spin a fantasy about how *A Cup of Joe* would have its premiere at the Chinese Theatre, and they'd ask me to write my name in the concrete. Did they do that with screenwriters? Probably not, but if they did, I'd do something incredibly clever, like press my forehead into the concrete—the font of my amazing creativity—the way Roy Rogers made an imprint of his revolver, and the kids from the *Harry Potter* movies pressed their wands.

Needless to say, I was feeling a little loopy. Maybe even *very* loopy—like, Heath-Ledger-in-*The-Dark-Knight* loopy.

I decided to go for a walk.

Down in the courtyard, I ran into someone on the way to the street.

"You must be Russel," she said. "Or is it Kevin?"

It was a woman—short, black, and nerdy. She had glasses with lenses that were too thick for her frames, a bit of an overbite, and cargo shorts that were pulled up a little too high. Basically, nothing quite fit. She was like the wrong lid on a piece of Tupperware.

Needless to say, I liked her instantly. I couldn't help glancing down at her shoes. Sure enough, she was wearing Onitsuka Tigers.

"Russel," I said. "But how—?"

"I'm Regina. Gina's girlfriend? She mentioned you to me. One of you is a screenwriter, right?"

"Oh!" I said. "Regina, huh? Gina and Regina?"

She rolled her eyes. "I know, how annoying. But I wanted to introduce myself, because there aren't many gay folks in this town, and we sorta have to look out for each other."

I stared at her.

"That was a joke," she said. "Because this town is, like, half gay?"

I laughed—maybe a little too much. "Yeah. Sorry, kind of slow here. So you're a comedian too?"

She made a face. "God, no! I'm not sure a couple can handle two comedians. I think that must be like two tops. There has to be someone to tell the joke, and there has to be someone else to laugh." This wasn't good. I'd known that Gina and Regina were a couple for all of ten seconds, and I was already sensing tension in their relationship.

"I'm a screenwriter too," she went on, and I couldn't help thinking about what Otto had said about the Screenwriter Loophole. Regina definitely looked the part. On the other hand, I hated that I'd been in town less than a week, and I was already putting people into boxes.

"Oh, that's great," I said. I desperately wanted to tell Gina the story of what was happening with Mr. Brander, in one big, long, firehose-like gush. But we'd only just met. Besides, it felt like bragging.

Instead I said, "What kind of things do you write?"

"Well, for a living, I wrote for reality TV for a while," she said.

I looked at her.

"Don't tell anyone," she said. "A lot of reality TV is scripted. But you probably already knew that."

"I actually didn't know that."

"Now I've done it, I've spoiled the illusion. We don't write the actual dialogue. We just set up the situations. Okay, you dragged it out of me: sometimes we *do* write dialogue. Everyone says, 'This is so fake, they should show the unedited footage.' But I've *seen* the unedited footage, and trust me, no one would want to watch that. Real 'reality' is actually quite boring."

"Don't take this the wrong way, but I think most reality TV is quite boring too."

Regina laughed. "Spoken like a writer of the *actual* scripted stuff. And I don't disagree. The longer I did it, the harder it was to escape the conclusion that reality TV is entertainment for stupid people."

"Oh, ouch!"

"What do you write?" she asked me.

Was this enough of an opportunity to tell her about the thing with Mr. Brander? I decided it was, so I (briefly, modestly) told her what was going on.

"Hey, congratulations!" she said, genuinely happy for me. "That's really, really great!" I'd told her about my experience with Fiona, so she also said, "Don't let that stuff with the agent bug you. Think about it from their point of view: it's a job to them. There are a zillion people who want to be screenwriters, but only a really small number of them are ever going to make any money. So they're just really, really, really selective. But I definitely know the vibe you're talking about. They make you feel like you're something on the bottom of their shoe. I think it's impossible to be a 'gatekeeper' without it going to your head. But hey, I can refer you to my agent if you want. Assuming she'll still take my calls."

"Really?" I said. Suddenly I was in *love* with the idea of calling Fiona Lang up and saying, "You know, you didn't seem very excited about my screenplay deal, so I've decided to go with another agent."

But that didn't seem quite right. She *had* agreed to rep this one deal, and I didn't want to get Otto in trouble. Regina had a point about everyone wanting a piece of a Hollywood agent, that it had to go to a person's head.

"I should probably wait and see how it goes with Fiona," I said. "But if it doesn't work out, I may take you up on that."

"Anyway, it was nice to meet you."

"Likewise!"

As I walked away from Regina, I suddenly remembered what Otto had told me: that living in Los Angeles, it was easy to meet other people in the industry.

He'd been so right. Literally all I'd had to do was set foot outside my door.

Later that afternoon, back in the apartment, I still hadn't heard from Fiona, and I was starting to feel like Heath Ledger's Joker again, so I decided to use the pool. Kevin was back now, and he came with me. Always before, we'd had the pool to ourselves. But this time, one of our neighbors was already there.

Daniel.

(Remember? The hot teenage neighbor we met before?)

He was floating on his back in the middle of the pool in a pair of black trunks. It was late in the afternoon now, so the deck was mostly in shade, but Daniel was still wearing dark glasses.

He looked great, of course. His trunks were skin-tight, not the baggy kind, and his body was lean and tan and ripped. I had a feeling Kevin was noticing him too, but it's not like we were going to stare.

Kevin and I put our towels on the deck chairs, kicked off our flip-flops, and slid down into the pool.

Daniel was right in front of us, still floating on his back. As we entered the pool, we basically came face-to-face with his crotch (face-to-crotch? Oy!). For someone so lean and muscled, Daniel was surprisingly buoyant, so we were definitely getting an eyeful. I'd thought before that he was wearing a pair of skin-tight trunks, but now I wondered if it wasn't just a pair of boxer briefs. The material seemed that thin and cotton-y.

At least I wasn't thinking about Fiona and Mr. Brander and the movie contract anymore. On the other hand, and maybe this is internalized homo-phobia on my part, I've always been annoyed by those gay guys who make a point to openly leer at other guys. A quick peek is one thing, but anything that makes the other person uncomfortable has always seemed like a dick-y thing to do, whether you're a straight guy ogling a woman or a gay guy ogling another guy. (Women rarely leer at all, which should tell us something right there.)

In the middle of the pool, Daniel bobbed in our wake. He slowly rotated away, so he was almost paral-lel to us now. At least we weren't staring directly at his crotch anymore, but unfortunately, he looked pretty good in silhouette too. I could see the waistband of his shorts now, the logo that read "Under Armour"—he was definitely wearing boxer-briefs.

Kevin caught me staring and gave me a knowing little smile.

I'd glanced over at Kevin at just the right time, because now Daniel looked over at us both. He scowled, I guess because we'd disturbed the water in "his" pool.

"Hey, there," Kevin said. "Daniel, right?"

He stared at us a second longer. Then he said, "Yup," over-emphasizing the "p," almost like he was making a popping sound.

*Well*, I thought, *at least now we know he speaks English.*

He settled back into the water like he was lying on a bed. He'd gone from looking annoyed to emanating complete boredom.

"So I guess you're in high school," Kevin said.

"Yup," he said, making the almost-pop with the "p" again.

"What, a senior?"

"Yup."

I couldn't help wondering how Daniel had ended up living with his sister, where their parents were.

"Hey," I said to Daniel, realizing something, "you must go to Hollywood High!" That was the local school where all these famous people went back in the seventies.

This time, he didn't even give me a "Yup," just stared at me blankly from behind his dark glasses, and I felt stupid for showing enthusiasm about anything in his presence. Did everyone in this damn town have attitude?

Done with Daniel, I faced Kevin. "So how was work?" I said.

"I spent four hours in the car in order to interview someone for fifteen minutes," Kevin said.

"That sucks."

"It's even worse. I'm not being paid by the hour."

From his side of the pool, Daniel said, "You're the gay guys, right?"

Slowly, almost in unison, we turned to look at him. We didn't say anything for a second, just stared at him.

Then, with perfect timing, Kevin said, "Yup," and of course he over-pronounced the "p." Kevin hated attitude too, but unlike me, he was much more willing to get back in people's faces. I stifled a laugh.

Daniel didn't react. Maybe he was too stupid to know he was being mocked.

I started to turn away again, determined to ignore him. The water sloshed and, I swear, it sounded exactly like someone slurping. I glanced back at Daniel—or, more specifically, to the thin, wet material clinging to his crotch.

This time, Daniel caught me looking. He smiled. Now I felt stupid.

"What about you?" Kevin asked me.

"Huh?" I said.

"No idea when you'll hear from Fiona?"

"Nah," I said. Unfortunately, he reminded me what I was trying so desperately to forget. I'd brought my phone to the pool, and I considered checking my email again.

As Kevin and I talked, Daniel must have been paddling with his hands, because he was suddenly back to floating in the exact middle of the pool. This wasn't a tiny swimming pool, but somehow Daniel was now taking up most of it— sort of like how a housecat, only three feet long, can somehow stretch out his body and take over almost all of an entire double bed.

Kevin looked at me and rolled his eyes.

Then he pushed off the wall backward into the water, making a big ripple across the pool.

Daniel went bobbing over to the other side. Once the center was clear, before Daniel could re-take it, Kevin moved in. I joined him, cheering him on with a mischievous grin.

Displaced as King of the Pool, Daniel sat upright in the water. Out of the corner of my eye, I could see him scowling at us, but we made a point of ignoring him again. I was tired of being tangled in the sticky web of this stupid kid.

"I have an idea for new screenplay though," I said to Kevin. "It's about this couple who inherits an old whiskey distillery, and they find this cache of old bottles. Little do they know that each bottle has an angry ghost trapped inside. It's called *Spirits*. Get it? It's about whiskey and it's about ghosts? 'Spirits'?"

"Clever. So it's a comedy?"

"Well, that's the thing. I can't decide. The title sort of sounds like a horror-comedy. But I'm thinking I might go straight horror."

As we were talking, Daniel faced the wall of the pool. He was right next to a metal ladder, and I expected him climb up it, but he ignored it, pulling his whole body onto the deck with one swift, impressive yank. It was sort of impossible not to stare at the muscles in his back, or the way the black boxer briefs clung to his pert round ass. He reminded me a little of a snake, with everything shifting in synch. Somehow I knew that Kevin was looking too.

Once on the deck, Daniel grabbed a towel and started drying off. He didn't turn away or anything. He stood right there on the deck, facing us, legs spread, the sun setting behind him, and slowly ran the towel back and forth behind his back. He was in silhouette again, the blue sky crisply outlining the shape of his body. But it was still afternoon, an hour or so from twilight, so the front of his body was visible too—the ridges in his stomach, the miles of smooth brown skin. He absolutely glistened.

Floating below him in the pool, I felt like a worshipper prostrate before the statue of some Mesoamerican sun god—maybe even Quetzalcoatl, the snake god.

*He knows we've been watching him*, I thought. We thought we'd vanquished him, but maybe he'd vanquished us. Had he just assumed we'd ogle him because we were two gay guys? That was a completely bigoted assumption! Okay, so, yeah, it happened to be totally spot-on. But it was still bigoted.

Daniel kept toweling off. Behind the wet, clinging material of those shorts, he jiggled.

*Okay, I give up*, I thought. *You win.*

"Daniel Manuel!" came a voice from the other side of the pool. "What do you think you're *doing*?"

It was Zoe, his older sister, arriving home from work.

Had she seen Kevin and me leering at her little brother? I felt stupid again. Then again, we hadn't really done anything wrong. Daniel had been a total dickhead. Yeah, Kevin and I had looked at him up on the deck, but that had been his whole *point*—to get us to look.

"How many times have I told you, you can't wear that in the pool!" Zoe went on.

"Chinga tu madre," Daniel said under his breath.

"What did you say to me?" Zoe said, louder, harsher.

"Nada, nada." Even in another language, I could tell Daniel was whining, exactly like a kid being caught eating the forbidden popsicles.

"Get over here right now!" Zoe said, and Daniel wrapped his towel around himself and scuttled her way, not unlike an admonished puppy. I guess she still had *some* control over him.

In a second, he was gone, thumping up the out-door steps that led to their apartment.

Zoe stayed behind, staring down at Kevin and me. I sort of expected her to apologize, to say she was sorry that Daniel had been wearing his underwear in the pool again.

But she didn't apologize. Now she glared at us, not hatefully like Daniel had done, but suspiciously, like we were puppies in need of admonishing too, or maybe something more serious than that—like we had something more serious to feel guilty about.

That was crazy. Like I said, Kevin and I hadn't done anything wrong. But I had a strange feeling this wasn't the last we were going to see of our annoying (and annoyingly hot) teenage neighbor.

# CHAPTER FIVE

I didn't hear from Fiona the next day, or the day after that. Then it was the weekend (when I didn't expect to hear from her), and I didn't hear from her on Monday either.

The next day, Tuesday, I met Otto for lunch again. Kevin had the car, so we ate at a place within walking distance of our apartment, an all-you-can-eat Indian buffet on Hollywood Boulevard.

"I'm paying," I said, before we headed to the buffet itself.

"What?" he said. "Why?"

"Because I owe you. You hooked me up with your agent."

"Is that all negotiated now?"

"No, but I'm sure it's just a matter of time."

"Everything always takes three times longer than they say it will," Otto said.

"Really?"

"Oh, yeah! It's another rule."

This actually made me feel better. I didn't know the first thing about how any of this worked.

We both loaded up at the buffet. Once we were

back at the table, Otto said, "So this Mr. Brander guy, he's the real deal, huh?"

"Well, he definitely *was* the real deal," I said. "I think that's why your agent took the project on—she knew the name at least. She was pretty upfront about the fact that he hasn't done anything in a long time. But that might end up helping us. I read online that no independent producer pays ten thousand bucks for an option on a spec script by an unknown writer anymore, not for a low budget project like this."

"Ten thousand bucks?" Otto said, and this time I sensed a note of jealousy in his voice. I couldn't blame him. He'd been working on his acting career for six years now, and he didn't have much to show for it. Meanwhile, I take up screenwriting a year ago, then I breeze into town, and two weeks later, I kinda sorta have a film in the works.

"I'm getting you a part in this movie," I said. "You know that, right?"

He nodded, but it was like he didn't quite believe me, or didn't think it would work out in the end.

"I'm serious," I said. "And, I mean, the movie probably won't get made anyway. The Internet was depressingly clear about that. Without financing, most options don't go anywhere."

"Russel," Otto said, stopping me, "I think it's great what happened to you. I really do. I'm bummed, but it's not about that."

"What's it about?"

"I had this audition yesterday. A real movie, not some indie piece of crap. And I was good. I'm not trying to brag, because God knows I've blown plenty of auditions. But I didn't blow this one. It may have been my best audition ever. I really got the character, and I don't know—I was just *on* right then.

"The producers thanked me," Otto said, "And they said all the right things: Wow, that was great, I loved what you did with the pencil, we'll let you know, blah, blah, blah. But just as I was walking out the door, I literally saw one of them drop my resume and headshot into the wastebasket. Ordinarily, I wouldn't have cared. I mean, they didn't think I was right for the part, so what? Maybe they had someone better, or maybe they'd already promised the part to the nephew of some investor. Them's the breaks, fine, whatever."

I nodded.

"But I *was* right for that part," Otto said. "I knew it in my bones. So I'm, like, hold the phone. I'd just given the best audition of my life. But they weren't considering me, they weren't even keeping my resume as a back-up in case none of the other actors were available. And I knew this wasn't about me not being right for the part or giving a bad audition. It was about my face. I felt like that dancer in that song from *A Chorus Line*. You know, where she grabs her score-card after an audition and sees that it reads, 'Dance: 10, Looks: 3'? But I'm not like that dancer—I can't go out and get plastic surgery and then come back and wow everyone with my fake tits. I've already *had* plastic surgery, and this"—he swept a hand over his face, his scars—"is as good as it gets."

"Which is pretty damn good," I said. "You're a totally handsome guy. Plus, you make references to *A Chorus Line*. What's not to like?"

Otto smiled, embarrassed.

83

"So I'm standing in the doorway of that audition," he went on, "and I wasn't sure what to do. I'd seen them dump my headshot in the trash, and I could also see it on their faces, that they'd already forgotten me, that they were moving on to whoever was next on their list. I knew I had absolutely nothing to lose, so I turned around and faced them and said, 'I'm right for this part. You all know I am.'"

"Really?" I said.

"Swear to God."

"What did they say?"

"They stared at me for a second. They weren't angry or annoyed—they almost looked scared. Definitely embarrassed. Which is how I knew for sure I was right about what was going on, why I'd been rejected. But no one wanted to come out and say it. So I closed the door behind me, and I said, 'Why couldn't this character have scars on his face? Why couldn't that be part of this movie?'"

"What did they say?" I said.

"They all sort of looked at each other. Then one of them said, 'Because it'll distract the audience. It's not what this movie is about.' So I said, 'But that's what's so great about it! It wouldn't be about the scar. It'd be completely incidental to the story. Think about the statement you'd be making!' And of course they said, 'We're not making a statement, we're making a movie.'"

"Assholes," I said.

"No, wait, hold on," Otto said. "When they said that, I thought that too. So I tried to argue with them. I said, 'You're not giving the audience enough credit. They're smarter than that. They'll understand what you're doing, they'll even give you credit for it!' And they said, 'Maybe they will, maybe they won't. It's a risk. But we've been working our butts off on this project for three years now. Somehow, incredibly, we finally got the money to make our movie. This is our one shot. If this movie is successful, we might get to make another movie. But if it's not, it could be years before we get another shot—if we *ever* get another shot. For us, everything is riding on this. And now here you come into our office, saying, 'This completely unrelated issue is really important to me, so important that I think you should risk *your* movie on it.' But we've already taken our risks—in the script, in our careers. This movie is one of the biggest risks the three of us have ever taken, because we've risked years of our lives to get it made.'"

As Otto had been talking, I'd been eating. Now I'd finished everything on my plate, but I wasn't going back to the buffet to load up again. Otto's story was too interesting.

Otto went on, still quoting the producers. "'You want the truth?' they asked me, and I nodded, and they said, 'You really were great today. If you didn't have that scar, we'd probably have seriously considered you. Even as it is, it'd be a really interesting choice to have a character who looked like you. If someone else made that movie, I'd totally support it. As for people with scars, I think there's way too much prejudice about stuff like that, and I look forward to a day when people change, when we all get more mature. But this is all still *your* issue. Everyone has issues they care about, things that are personal to them, and that's yours. We're just not willing to risk our whole careers on *your* issue. If you want to take that risk, you should make your own movie.'"

When he was done, Otto stared at me. He wasn't done with his plate yet—he'd been talking, so he'd barely touched his food.

"Wow," I said. "But look, just because those guys—"

"No, wait, hold the phone," Otto said, stopping me. "Don't you see? I finally get it. It's not just those guys. It's everyone. They didn't say anything offensive. They were just being honest. I asked, and they told me the truth. And they're right. If I were them, I'd probably see it exactly the same way. That's what most people don't know about this town, about Hollywood. Everyone always talks like Hollywood is, like, one thing, one entity. But it's not. It's a bunch of people, individuals. And just by coming here, we've all taken the biggest risk there is: we've risked our whole lives. The competition is beyond insane, success is a total pipe-dream, and we're all only hanging on by our fingernails. If one of us does break through, if we do find ourselves in a position of power for five minutes, we know we're only a flop or two away from being thrown out on our ass."

I didn't say anything to that. What could I say?

"I'm not trying to be Debbie Downer," Otto said.

"Really?" I said. "Because what would you be like if you *did* try?"

Otto half-snorted. "I'm just discouraged." He played with his food with his fork. "Right after I nailed that audition, I was actually thinking I might've finally got my break. That's what this town does to you: it leads you on. It's like a slot machine. It delivers just enough winnings to keep you going. And all around you, people are hitting jackpots, bright lights and bells and everything. But you never win. It slowly whittles you down."

"You know, I really *am* getting you a part in my movie," I said.

"Don't take this the wrong way, but..."

"What?"

"You're the writer," Otto said. "No one listens to the writer about anything."

I'd heard this before—the old joke about the starlet who was so stupid that she slept with the writer in order to advance her career.

"Mr. Brander's different," I said. "You should've heard him."

"I know," he said. "I just...need something more definite. I'm getting to the end of my rope." He nodded to my empty plate, even as he finally started digging into his own. "Go get more food."

I did get more food, mostly because I needed time to ponder everything he'd told me. Otto was thinking about giving up acting? That made me feel even more guilty than before, that my break had come so easy with Mr. Brander. It was almost too good to be true.

By the time I made it back from the buffet, I'd come up with the perfect solution.

I put my plate on the table and said, "What about what those producers said? Why not make your own movie?"

Otto stirred his food. "Yeah, I thought about that too. But you still need money. Even a micro-budget is, like, fifty thousand dollars. And I don't have a screenplay or anything."

"*I'll* write the screenplay. And what about Kickstarter? That seems like exactly the kind of thing people might actually donate to, a movie with a cause."

"Russel, you don't..." But then he stopped. "Hold the phone, what about a web series?" He was thinking out loud now. "I know someone who has a camera— if it's only online, we don't need, like, a Redbox or anything. I know someone who can direct it. And I can handle the editing, nothing too crazy."

He looked back at me, his face breaking into a big grin. I was about to say, "What should we write it about?" But before I could, Otto said, "I could write it about my own experience, about being an actor with a scar. I know there are a zillion web series about people trying to make it in Hollywood, but I've never seen anything like *my* story. Have you?"

I shook my head no.

"I could call it, like...*Scarface*," Otto said.

"That's good," I said, nodding.

Truthfully, I was a little disappointed Otto didn't want me to write his web series. He probably hadn't even heard my offer. But he was probably right that it should tell his own story—and he'd be better writing that than I would. Besides, this lunch had been about cheering Otto up. Whatever I'd done, it had worked: he was shoveling up his food in big bites. It was nice to have done something for him for a change.

"Are you going back?" I said, meaning the buffet.

"Hells to the yes," he said. "Aren't you?"

"Sure."

"But afterward I wanna take you somewhere. Shoe shopping."

"Oh," I said. "Okay, thanks."

"As a thank you for today."

"You don't need to buy me—"

Otto stopped me with a quick smile. "Oh, I'm not *buying*. The thank you is helping you shop. And you're still picking up lunch. You're the one with the freakin' ten thousand dollar option!"

I laughed and said, "Fair enough."

It wasn't until the following week that I finally heard from Fiona.

Fifteen fucking days after we talked on the phone.

I could describe the rest of those days for you, but that would probably drive you as crazy as it did me. What kind of crazy comes after Heath Ledger in *The Dark Knight*? Bill O'Reilly in real life? Anyway, that was me. I checked my iPhone so often, I probably almost broke it. But finally an email arrived from Fiona:

**Contract attached. Print four copies, sign, and send all four to me. I'll send you a copy once all are counter-signed. Call with questions.**

I knew I was a newbie, but wasn't it typical for the client to be *consulted* before finalizing a contract? And I hadn't exactly expected a fruit basket and a bottle of champagne from Fiona, but a phone call might have been nice.

I opened up the contract and was confronted by sixteen pages of mostly incomprehensible legal mumbo-jumbo. But I definitely understood the words "ten thousand dollars" in the section marked "Option." And if the movie actually got made at a budget of six million (as Mr. Brander had said), I stood to make another whopping hundred and forty thousand dollars (two and a half percent of the total production budget, minus the option money, up to a "ceiling" of two-fifty). Plus, I had five percent of "net profits," which even I knew that, due to creative Hollywood accounting, was basically meaningless. (Supposedly, the producers of the *Star Wars*, *Spider-Man*, and *Harry Potter* movies—some of the most popular films in history—are arguing that they still haven't turned any profits.) But like everyone who's ever gotten net points on a movie, I could at least *imagine* that the movie would be so successful that I'd someday get a check for two million dollars.

My first official movie deal, and it was now officially done. So why was I so uneasy about it? I thought about emailing Fiona back and asking if she'd had a chance to read my screenplays yet, but I wasn't even close to being ready to have her write back to say, "Yes, and I thought they were dreadful."

Feeling superstitious, I quickly printed out four copies of the contract, signed them, and then ran out to the nearest post office to send them off. When I got home, Kevin was back from another interview.

"I got the contract!" I said. "It's already signed and off to the agent."

"Seriously?" Kevin said. "That's fantastic!" He kissed me. "Now we have to go out and celebrate."

The contract may have been signed, but we didn't have the check yet, and it was only going to be for eight thousand five hundred anyway (after Fiona's fifteen percent commission). So unfortunately, "celebrate" just meant chicken and waffles at the Hollywood Roscoe's.

But there was a concert that night at the Hollywood Bowl, which is only about a half mile away from our apartment, and walking home you could hear the music flowing out through the whole neighborhood—some kind of jazz instrumental. Meanwhile, the night was cool and the sky was a vibrant indigo. For once, the air smelled more like the sea and the plants of the Hollywood hills than it did exhaust from all the freeways.

When we got back to the apartment, the second we were inside the door, Kevin turned to me and took me into his arms.

"I thought you needed to email your writer," I said. This was something he'd talked about at dinner.

"Fuck my writer," he said, kissing me.

I resisted the obvious joke about how I'd rather fuck him (and maybe vice-versa). I was too busy kissing him back.

Then we were undressing, even as we were heading toward the bedroom, hopping on one foot and then the other, leaving a trail of discarded clothing behind us just like in the movies.

By the time we reached the bed, we were down to our underwear, both of us tenting big-time.

I worked my way down to his grey boxer-briefs, to the considerable bulge I found there.

"Unleash the Kraken!" I said to Kevin, who laughed as I yanked his underwear down around his thighs. His dick popped upright with the fury of a battering ram.

The Kraken had definitely been unleashed, and I spent at least the next hour wrestling it down.

\* \* \*

I woke up later that night. It was darker out, but I figured we couldn't have been asleep that long, because I could still hear the concert from the Hollywood Bowl.

*No*, I thought. *Something's not right.*

I glanced at the clock. It was 2:07 a.m. So it couldn't be the concert—that had to be long over by now. The music sounded different anyway. That had been jazz, loose and contemporary. This was tighter, more melodic, brassier—big band, like something from the 1950s. Maybe it was one of the neighbors playing music, or even someone from the sidewalk outside. Except it didn't sound like it was coming from outside. It sounded like it was coming from right inside the apartment.

*Did we leave the music on?* I thought. But we'd started kissing the second we entered the apartment. Did Kevin get up after we fell asleep? I didn't think we had any music like this. Maybe it was some new ringtone of his, or the television.

The music didn't stop, just kept playing, big and brassy.

I looked over at Kevin, wheezing softly, sound asleep next to me. There was no reason to wake him, so I pulled on my underwear and t-shirt and slipped out of bed.

I could still hear the music. It had to be the concert at the Bowl—some after-hours party. Except I couldn't believe the city would allow that. Plus, it still didn't sound like it was coming from outside.

I stepped into the front room. The music wasn't

loud, but somehow it really did sound like it was coming from inside the apartment. It had to be a trick of the acoustics—something to do with the night air, or the apartment, or both. It was probably the neighbors. It did sort of sound like a radio, one of the old-fashioned kind that you had to tune, that fade in and out. The Venetian blinds were down but open, and the windows were open too. Light spilled in past the vertical slats, casting bar-like shadows. It wasn't moonlight, just the omnipresent glow of the city at night. The trail of Kevin's and my discarded clothing was still there, everything exactly the way we'd left it. But then why wouldn't it be?

I started to turn back to the bedroom, but something stopped me.

My skin tingled, the first touch of a masseuse.

*I'm not alone*, I thought.

I turned back toward the front room, but it was empty, completely still. The music played on.

I tensed. Did we have an intruder? But I didn't tense that much, because it didn't feel like that kind of presence. It didn't feel dangerous. It felt like whoever was there *belonged* there.

I thought about that night before, the day we'd been unpacking, when I'd imagined I'd seen those ghosts from the past. But those had been fantasies, fleeting flights of fancy. This felt different. Maybe I was still asleep and dreaming.

*"There's even supposed to be a ghost."* That's what Gina had said about our apartment.

That was ridiculous. There was no such thing as ghosts. But I was suddenly a lot more sympathetic toward people who claimed to sense them. Now I knew what it felt like, how your skin prickled, and your hands and feet went cold. For a second, I thought about going back into the bedroom to wake Kevin. I hadn't even closed the door behind me—I could still hear him breathing. I wasn't sure what he'd think though. And if I went to get Kevin, I wasn't sure the presence would still be here when we got back.

"Hello?" I whispered.

The music stopped. Had it stopped abruptly, someone turning a switch, or had it just come to the end of the song? I couldn't tell. I'd been listening for an answer to my question, not listening closely to the music. But did it even matter if it had stopped suddenly, if I'd only been overhearing the neighbor's radio?

Outside the windows, the freeway hissed.

*There's no one here,* I thought. It was just like before, that night I'd imagined the past, but this time, I'd let my imagination get away from me.

I turned back for the bedroom, then realized I needed to use the bathroom first.

Halfway across the room, a male voice said, urgently, "Whatever you do, don't—"

I turned back for the bedroom, hoping that Kevin would be standing in the doorway, warning me that I was about to stub my toe on a table or something.

He wasn't there.

Maybe it was another trick of the acoustics, another noise from the neighbor's apartment?

It didn't sound like that. As with the music, it had sounded like it was *in* the apartment with me, in the same room I was in. But the voice had sounded a little like a radio too, like it had to be tuned. We were together, but also somehow not.

What was I not supposed to do? The voice had faded away before he could say.

I was scared, but not because of the presence: I didn't feel any sense of danger from that. No, it was more the urgency of the warning. It seemed like it was directed at me, that it was really important I hear it.

"Don't do what?" I said to the room, to the presence.

It didn't answer.

"Please," I said. "Tell me."

There was still no answer.

Suddenly I felt like an idiot. Of course I hadn't heard anything real. I probably wasn't fully awake or something. If there had been music and a voice, it was just a radio. It had even sounded like that. Why in the world would I assume it was a ghost trying to communicate with me from across the dimensions?

I used the bathroom and went back to bed, cuddling up to Kevin, who never did wake up. I didn't care that the room was stuffy, and his body was sweaty. I'd already decided I wasn't going to tell him what I thought I'd experienced. I felt stupid enough about it already.

But I didn't drift off to sleep, not until even deeper in the night. I couldn't shake the feeling that the voice and its warning had been real, that it had been meant for me, and that I was somehow about to make the biggest mistake of my life.

# CHAPTER SIX

Everybody makes a big deal about the first time you have sex, and it *is* a big deal, mostly because you don't really know what to expect. But don't people *kinda sorta* know what to expect, at least these days? I mean, it's not like we live in Victorian times where people haven't ever seen another person naked. Most teenagers have seen plenty of sex online. Even if "porn" isn't exactly the same thing as "sex," people still have a general idea of what goes where with who.

The following Monday, Lewis called and invited me over to Mr. Brander's house for the very first *A Cup of Joe* development meeting. It was scheduled for the next day.

Unlike sex for a virgin, I had *absolutely no idea* what to expect.

I'm not a complete idiot: I assumed that "developing" a project meant figuring out how to turn the screenplay into an actual movie. It's not like they're the same thing. So I assumed we'd talk about a director, and the budget, and locations, and casting, and probably also what was wrong with the script itself, what needed revising. But exactly what did all that involve? And who would *be* involved? Just Mr. Brander, Lewis, and me?

When I was still on the phone with him, I thought about asking Lewis what to expect, but I figured that would paint me as even more of a total newbie, so I decided not to.

Basically, for the second time in my life, I was a fumbling, awkward, blushing virgin. And I had no choice but to drop trou, clench my teeth, and get the damn thing over.

Once again, I was determined to be at Mr. Brander's house early, and once again, thanks to the horrible traffic, I just barely made it (and, of course, at one point I was almost killed).

Still embarrassed by my car, I parked along the street and let Lewis buzz me in on foot.

He met me at the front door.

"Lewis," I said.

"Russel," he said.

There was something different about him this time, but I couldn't figure out what it was. It wasn't his shoes or his clothing, which I'm pretty sure were exactly the same as before.

"What's up?" I said.

He was looking away. "This way."

I could hear voices behind him in the front room. Rather than being decorated with movie posters and photos and awards like Mr. Brander's office, this room was filled with antiques: fixtures with crystal beads and pots made of hammered brass, even a big carved wood fireplace mantle. The curtains dripped with tassels, and the couches were mostly of the "divan" type. The area smelled like dried flowers, something vaguely sweet and a little like hay.

I stepped into the grand arch of the entryway. Mr. Brander wasn't there, but there were four people—three men and a woman, all seated. For a second, no one noticed me, so I took the opportunity to scan their shoes. They all looked nice—various shades of leather—but even after going shopping with Otto, I still didn't know anything about shoes, so I decided then and there that I needed to stop checking them out.

By now, people were noticing me, and noticing Lewis standing next to me, like I was someone important, like he was about to introduce me. Weirdly, once again, I wasn't that nervous.

"This is Russel," Lewis said to the gathering. "The screenwriter of *A Cup of Joe?*"

Everyone smiled and talked at once, complimenting me and telling me how much they liked the script. I knew they were probably just being polite, that it was mostly a lot of hot air, completely insincere, but I confess: I definitely liked insincere hot air better than the cold indifference of Fiona Lang.

Then someone said, "I especially liked the flashbacks."

Someone else, "Oh! Yeah, that wasn't what I was expecting," and everyone else agreed with him.

*Maybe they're not just being polite*, I thought.

Lewis went around the room introducing them: Evan, the casting director, tall and slouchy, with a nervous edge; Andrea, the line producer, in a baseball cap and ponytail, somehow a little too enthusiastic;

Bryce, the co-producer, an aging surfer-dude type with a bristly grey goatee and premature wrinkles; and finally, Justin, the associate producer, a surprisingly buff Asian guy of indeterminate age, the calmest of us all.

Except for casting director, I didn't know what any of those titles meant.

Part of me was relieved. Like I said, I was worried it was going to be just Mr. Brander, Lewis, and me. Either that or it would be a bunch of old people—all the people Mr. Brander had worked with before, away from the retirement home for the day. I had a really hard time imagining that anyone would take this film project seriously if it was being put together by a bunch of people with walkers and cataracts.

These people all looked like the real thing, ready to get moving. Evan and Justin had iPads, and Andrea clutched a pen and clipboard.

"Can I get you something to drink?" Lewis asked me. There were already drinks set on stone coasters all around the room.

"Evian?" I said, a little pleased with myself that I already sounded slightly less pathetic than before.

"Sure thing," Lewis said, and he left to go get it.

I took a seat. Now it was just me and the other producers, and there was this sort of awkward moment when everyone was staring at me. Which I guess made sense: I'd written the screenplay that was the reason why everyone had gathered there.

It seemed like it was up to me to say something, so I said the kind of thing you say at a party: "How do you guys know Mr. Brander?"

There was another awkward moment.

"I just met him last week!" Andrea said.

"Me too," Bryce said.

"Friend of a friend of a friend," Justin said.

"I mean, I'd *heard* of him," Evan said. "But yeah."

Silence descended yet again. So I said, "An old house? None of us have met before, and none of us know the host? Sounds like we've all been invited by an eccentric billionaire to spend the night in a haunted mansion."

Everyone laughed—*really* laughed—and I felt great. I was totally killing this "development meeting" thing.

*Making it in Hollywood?* I thought. *This isn't so hard!*

Everyone was still looking at me, smiling, so I went on to say, "In the end, of course, we'll discover we were all somehow responsible for the death of Mr. Brander's daughter five years ago."

No one laughed this time, and I realized I'd killed the joke.

*Okay, so maybe this isn't so easy.* At least I could still fall back on the Screenwriter Loophole. If people *expected* the screenwriter to be a total loser, maybe I wasn't doing that bad.

"But what a list of credits, huh?" I said, forging onward. "I mean, who *hasn't* Mr. Brander worked with?"

"He told me how he worked with Jack Lemmon," Evan said.

"Ha!" Andrea said. "He told me about working with Debbie Reynolds."

"Sean Connery," Stuart said.

"Bette Davis," Justin said.

So now I knew how Mr. Brander got people to work with him: he name-dropped. Mr. Brander had done the same thing with me, with Tennessee

Williams and also Bette Davis. (I couldn't help but think: *Justin is gay too? I mean, Bette Davis, come on.*)

Before long, people started talking about their own projects.

"I was working with Lisa Kudrow and Dan Bucatinsky on this project," Bryce said, "and Don Roos, of course."

"Of course," someone said as if it was obvious.

*Why is that obvious?* I thought.

"I really like *Web Therapy*!" Andrea said.

"Do you?" Evan said. "Because I feel like it doesn't always come together. I mean, I'd watch Lily Tomlin read the phone book. But that's sort of what it feels like sometimes, Lily Tomlin reading the phone book."

Everyone grunted in agreement, and I did too, even though I'd never seen *Web Therapy*.

"I've been involved with this thing with Tim Burton and Jake Gyllenhaal over at Searchlight," Andrea said.

Everyone murmured their approval.

"I've been working with Jonah Hill on this screenplay he wrote," Justin said.

"*Pure Imagination* at Sony?" Evan said.

"No," Justin said. "That one's finally truly dead, even though Jonah won't admit it. This is something else. I know actors always think they can write, and they can't, but this guy really can."

Listening to all this, I was totally impressed. Then I remembered what Otto had said about the Bullshit Factor, how everyone supposedly exaggerated their credits and accomplishments by a factor of three in order to make themselves sound better. Did that mean Bryce wasn't really working with Lisa Kudrow, and Andrea hadn't set anything up at Searchlight, and

Justin didn't even know Jonah Hill? If they'd done all those things, knew all those people, why were they working with someone like Mr. Brander, someone who hadn't made a movie in more than twenty years? But if everyone in this town was always bullshitting about everything (even their shoes), how could you tell anything about anyone? I had to remember to ask Otto that.

At some point, Lewis returned with my Evian and a glass of ice. I barely had a chance to thank him before he disappeared again.

"What about you?" someone asked me.

"What?" I said.

"What are you working on?" It was Evan. He looked genuinely interested, not like he was trying to put me on the spot.

Everyone was looking at me again.

I could have told the truth and said, "This is the first thing I've ever done with anyone." But then I thought: *No. If everyone bullshits in Hollywood, then I need to bullshit too.*

So I said, "You guys know a writer named Vernie Rose? She was nominated for an Oscar a few years back. Anyway, she and I were working on this project together, but then Isaac called me about this."

This wasn't entirely a lie. I actually did know a screenwriter named Vernie Rose (my mentor back in Seattle), and she *had* been nominated for an Oscar. But it had been back in the 1970s, in Short Film not Feature, and Vernie was retired now. She'd read all of my screenplays so far, and given me great notes—she was the one who'd suggested the high school flashbacks in *A Cup of Joe* in the first place—but she and I hadn't ever even talked about working together.

Everyone kept looking at me, and I totally expected someone to say something like, "Vernie Rose? You liar! She's not still writing screenplays! Besides, that Oscar nomination was only for Short Film!"

But no one did. People just nodded and smiled and grunted, as if I'd impressed them.

*This really* isn't *so hard!* I thought. *I can totally do this!* I hadn't even needed to rely on the Screenwriter Loophole.

Even so, I didn't want to spend the whole afternoon telling lies, so I decided to change the subject.

"This is a great old house," I said. "I love that fireplace."

"You should see the bathroom!" Andrea said. "I think there's an actual leopard skin cover on the toilet seat."

"There is *not*," Justin said. "This I have to see."

"Seriously. I didn't even want to touch it."

"Oh, you should always put the lid down before you flush it," Evan said.

"My boyfriend *never* puts the seat down," Andrea said.

"Not the seat," Evan said. "The lid! The seat is a different issue. If you don't put the lid down before you flush, it sends all these *particles* up into the air."

"Are you really saying what I think you're saying?" Justin said to Evan. "About flushing the toilet?"

"*Fecal* particles," Evan said. "Yes, I'm really saying it. And it's true. There've been studies."

"That is *disgusting*," I said, and everyone laughed.

"I can't believe we're talking about this," Justin said, but he was laughing when he said it.

"Andrea brought it up!" Evan said. "She started talking about the toilet seat."

"I was talking about the seat *cover*," Andrea said. "I didn't say anything about *fecal particles*!"

Everyone laughed again, even me.

The point to all this isn't just that I was totally rocking this development meeting, not coming across like a total newbie at all. It's also that those producers and I were actually having fun. I liked them, and (even more important than their liking my screenplay), they seemed to like *me*.

"Well," said a voice that resounded from the doorway, "it sounds like I'm missing the party."

Mr. Brander, who clearly knew something about acoustics.

We all stopped in mid-laugh and looked over at him.

He was sitting there, perfectly positioned in the middle of the arch. He looked absolutely relaxed in his wheelchair—Abraham Lincoln looking out from his memorial. It was the perfect entrance—he totally owned the room—and I went back to being reminded of some movie about an eccentric billionaire inviting guests to spend the night in his haunted mansion.

Mr. Brander rolled forward and took a spot in front of us, and I realized there was no area rug on the floor, and that the furniture had been arranged in such a way that there was an open spot for his wheelchair. But we were definitely not the Knights of the Round Table. Somehow, imperceptibly, Mr. Brander had ended up on one side of the room with everyone else facing him.

Lewis stood behind him in the hallway, wordless, watching.

Mr. Brander didn't say anything for a second

either. He looked at us, going around in a circle, taking us in, the courtiers to the king.

"Welcome," Mr. Brander said at last. "I'm so pleased you could all come. Every movie tells a story, and every story begins with an opening shot—the opening scene. In a good movie, that scene tells you something important about the story, maybe the *most important* thing about the story: it sets the tone. But it also foreshadows the ending." He looked at me. "As every writer can tell you, the ending to a good story is usually found at the very beginning." He winked. "But never in the way the audience expects, right?" I smiled, and Mr. Brander turned back to the whole group. "But the making of a movie is a story too, with a beginning, a middle, and an end. With a protagonist"—here he nodded to all of us—"and rising tension, and plenty of obstacles along the way, all leading to a resolution that is satisfying to everyone involved. So let's set the tone, shall we? This is our opening scene. What does it tell us about our resolution? What hints and secrets are evident in this gathering that we've barely taken notice of, but that will have great and obvious importance in retrospect? Only time will tell, yes? But mark my words, everything we say here today, everything we do, will make perfect sense when we look back. And so we begin."

Even at the time, some part of me knew this was a cheesy, over-the-top speech—that Mr. Brander had probably given it a dozen times before, maybe at the beginning of every movie he'd ever set out making. But it didn't *sound* cheesy, not at all. He absolutely sold it. It also didn't sound rehearsed. Like any good speech, it sounded new, fresh, like the words, the insights, were coming to him right then on a direct line from God.

"Russel?" Mr. Brander said. "Why don't you start? Why don't you tell us what led you to write *A Cup of Joe*?"

"You expect me to follow *that*?" I said.

This got another huge laugh from everyone in the room, Mr. Brander and Lewis included. It was even bigger than my joke about how Mr. Brander was an eccentric billionaire who had invited us all to spend the night in his haunted mansion.

With my opening joke landing so great, I could totally take it from there. I told everyone what Mr. Brander and I had talked about before—how we saw the script, what it meant, how I hoped people would respond.

After that, Mr. Brander outlined the next step in the process: raising the money we needed (still six million dollars). In a nutshell, he and the other producers had to find development money, which would enable them to attach name actors, which would then allow them to make "pre-sales" to various distributors and territories, which would also enable them to approach various corporate entities for equity financing. He also wanted to at least explore product placement, and they would resort to supergap financing only as a very last resort.

I understood almost none of this, so let me nutshell it for you:

THEY WERE GOING TO MAKE A FUCKING MOVIE OUT OF MY FUCKING SCREENPLAY!

Before I knew it, we were finished. I'd made it through my first development meeting. I was no longer a virgin. The truth is, it was even more like sex than I'd thought: it had hardly been painful at all.

And I'd had a total blast.

I didn't go straight home after the meeting. For one thing, it was later in the day now—the middle of rush hour—so traffic was even more horrible than before (as if that's possible). So I decided to stop at the library.

I never had told Kevin about my encounter with the "ghost." I was too embarrassed. I still didn't really think it had been real. It had just been some weird trick of the acoustics, or maybe I really had been sleepwalking. At the same time, I'd been genuinely curious about that supposed suicide in our apartment all those years ago. I'd researched it on the computer at home (when Kevin wasn't around), but I hadn't found anything, so I'd come to the library to see what I could discover.

Since it was late afternoon, it was mostly mothers with their kids in the library, plus a handful of scruffy people sitting at the computer terminals, a few of whom were obviously looking at porn. I was the only white person—everyone else, including the librarians, was black or Latino, something that was still taking a little getting used to after living in Seattle.

I walked up to the guy at the research desk.

"I heard a rumor there was a suicide in my apartment," I told him. "I wanted to find out if it's true. I don't know when it happened, but it was a long time ago—like, maybe fifty years."

He thought for a second. "I'd start with the

newspaper archive," he said. "But search for the address. A lot of apartment buildings have changed their names over the years."

So (after waiting twenty minutes) I sat down at one of the computers dedicated to the newspaper archive. I was basically searching the entire twentieth century, so I obviously got a lot of returns. I tried to narrow things down. I quickly discovered that newspapers almost never referred to deaths as "suicides," at least not in obituaries or news articles.

Finally, I found a short mention in the "Notices" section of a newspaper dated August 11th, 1950. The librarian had been right, and the name of the apartment had since been changed:

**Cole Gordon was found dead last night in his room at 1189 Ivar Avenue, the Rising Sun Apartments, police said. Gordon, 34, was an unproduced screenwriter.**

*So it's true?* I thought. Except I still didn't know that he'd killed himself. When I searched for "suicide" and "Cole Gordon," nothing came up. I didn't even know if he'd lived in Kevin's and my actual apartment.

I did find Cole Gordon's obituary, which was printed a couple of days later.

**Cole Gordon was born January 12, 1915, in Dayton, Ohio, and died in his apartment in Hollywood, August 10, 1950. He was single. He was survived by his parents, A.J. and Sara Gordon, and a brother, Edgar Gordon, of Huber Heights, Ohio. Funeral services will be held at**

**the Taylorsville Mennonite Church, Huber Heights, Ohio, August 15, 2 pm. Interment will be made in the adjoining cemetery.**

There was also a picture. Cole Gordon had thick dark hair greased back in the suggestion of a pompadour. He wasn't particularly handsome—he had a beakish nose and glasses so thick they magnified his eyes. There was a hint of a smile, but only a hint. He looked like an adult posing for a high school yearbook.

*That's him*, I thought. *That's the person I heard that night.*

Or was it? Maybe my recognizing him was all in my mind—it probably was. But he did seem familiar somehow.

Had he really killed himself? The newspaper still didn't say, but why else would someone that young have died in his apartment? If he'd been in a car crash, he would have died on the scene of the accident, or later in the hospital. If he'd had some kind of illness, he probably would have died in a hospital too. A suicide was the only thing that made any sense.

*Gordon, 34, was an unproduced screenwriter.*

So he'd moved to Hollywood just like I had, to make it as a screenwriter, maybe even around the same age I was, twenty-four. Ten years later, he was still unproduced. Was it really so crazy to imagine him killing himself?

It's tempting to look at a picture of someone who's committed suicide and imagine you can see hints of the tragedy in their face. But that's stupid. It was one photo, one instant in a life that surely contained plenty of happy moments, along with the obvious sad ones.

So I was probably projecting. But I *did* see tragedy on his face. I could see it in the tightness of his lips, a sadness in those magnified eyes that his forced smile couldn't disguise.

When this picture was taken, had Cole Gordon known the demons were coming for him? I guess it didn't matter, because one way or another, they'd caught up with him in the end.

# CHAPTER SEVEN

Two days later, Kevin and I were both at home working—Kevin on an interview with some reality TV star, me on *Spirits*—when there was a knock on our apartment door. I was at the desk with the computer in the front room, and he was in the kitchen with the laptop.

For a second, we both sat there looking across the apartment at each other, like that knock on the door didn't quite compute. We'd been in Los Angeles for over a month now, and this was literally the first time anyone had ever knocked on our door.

I answered it. It was Daniel.

"Oh," I said, surprised. "Hey. What's up?"

He was back to wearing clothes—khaki pants with the pockets out again and a polo shirt, rumpled and grubby. Up close, he was a little shorter than I expected, five-eight, or maybe even five-seven. He looked slightly less bored than usual, peering beyond me into the apartment.

"So this is where you guys live, huh?" he said.

"Um, yeah."

Somehow—I'm not quite sure how—he pushed

past me and stepped inside. He looked around like a landlord, seeing how we'd arranged the furniture, taking in the posters on the walls, and my collection of *Lord of the Rings* Pez dispensers. He came to my keys and wallet on a bureau by the door. He noticed me noticing him notice it, and nodded and half-laughed at me, like he was saying, "Don't worry, dude, I'm not gonna steal your damn wallet."

Kevin stood in the doorway to the kitchen, watching it all.

"Hola," Daniel said to him.

"What's up?" Kevin said.

"Nada," Daniel said, continuing his inspection, picking up one of Kevin's baseballs (signed by Ichiro Suzuki), almost sniffing it like a cat. "I just wanna see where you guys live."

Kevin looked at me, but I shrugged. I didn't know what the hell this was about any more than he did. Daniel had been such a preening jackass that day in the pool that it didn't make any sense he'd visit us in our apartment.

"Well," I said, and I was about to go on to say, "we should get back to work," when Daniel flopped down on our couch. He didn't quite put his feet up on the coffee table, but he leaned back with this whole relaxed demeanor like he was planning on staying a while. He opened the case on my iPad mini (and for one brief moment, I was terrified that I'd left it open to a page of porn, but was glad to remember it was password protected).

I'd said that Mr. Brander had owned that room during the development meeting, and he had, but Daniel was somehow owning this room too. This was *my actual apartment*, and I doubted I'd ever looked as relaxed as he did at that moment. The self-confidence of this kid was amazing. Right then, it was alternating in my mind between really annoying and really attractive.

"So what's it like," he said, "living here, just two guys?"

I looked to Kevin again. That sounded suspiciously like Daniel was asking us what it was like to be gay.

"It's all good," Kevin said. "Uh, shouldn't you be in school?"

"No school today," he said.

*Right,* I thought. Part of me wanted to say, "Do you have any idea how much more difficult your life is going to be if you don't finish high school?" But I was annoying myself even by thinking it. Besides, maybe he had a good reason to be here. Maybe he had questions about himself, we were the only gay people he knew, and he'd come here for advice.

I took a seat across from him, and Kevin sat on my armrest. It's not like either of us was going to come out and ask him, "Do you think you might be gay?" We both knew that was something you shouldn't ever say to a teenager. The whole point was to let them tell you in their own time, even if it seemed like they were begging to be asked.

"Where's your sister?" Kevin asked.

"Work," he said.

"Does she know you're here?"

He cocked an eyebrow. "She don't ever know where I am. Besides, she don't like you guys."

How could she not like us? She didn't even know us.

"Why doesn't she like us?" I said.

He lifted the other eyebrow, like it was obvious.

*She thinks we're going to hit on her brother!* This actually pissed me off. It's true we'd noticed him, how he looked, that he was a cute guy. But looking was a lot different from touching. Besides, he was only seventeen years old. Plus, Kevin and I were monogamous—we didn't fuck around with other people. If we ever did, it definitely wouldn't be with some openly cocky, but secretly confused teenager.

Now I was torn. On one hand, I wanted Daniel to leave—he was annoying, and Kevin and I both had work to do. On the other hand, he might still have questions about himself.

"You want something to drink?" I asked Daniel.

"Sure," he said. "Got a Corona?"

"Uh, how about a Coke?"

He shrugged, and I went into the kitchen and tossed him a can.

Daniel drank it while picking at the padding on the sole of his shoe.

"So what's up?" Kevin said.

Daniel shrugged.

*Work with us*, I thought. *You came to us.*

"You need help with school?" Kevin said. "'Cause Russel here is pretty smart."

"Thanks a lot," I said, whacking him on the arm. I looked at Daniel. "But Kevin's right. If you need help with anything, *Kevin* would be glad to give it a go. I'm just kidding. We both would."

I expected him to scoff or shrug or roll his eyes, but he actually sort of smiled. "Cool," he said. He really was adorable, even with all that attitude: thick, wavy, coal black hair, probably parted with his fingers, and great olive skin.

Suddenly I sort of saw things from Zoe's point of view. She didn't know us, but she had to know that Daniel was a good-looking guy. She also had to see how people looked at him—probably both women and men, especially in Los Angeles. And I'm sorry to say this, but Daniel didn't seem like the sharpest crayon in the box. It wasn't hard to imagine a situation where someone took advantage of those two interrelated facts.

Daniel's eyes searched the floor. The can of Coke twisted in his hands.

"I have these...*questions*," he said. "Not about school. About...me."

Almost imperceptibly, Kevin and I leaned in closer. It felt like the universe was holding its breath, but maybe it was just Kevin and me.

Daniel burst out laughing.

"¡Chingados!" he said. "¡Ustedes creen que soy maricón!"

At first I didn't understand. But I didn't need to speak Spanish to figure out that he was laughing at us—that he'd somehow sensed what we were thinking, that we thought he might be gay and have questions for us, so he'd played us. Again.

*Okay*, I thought. *Maybe Daniel's not so stupid.*

Still laughing, Daniel stood up and breezed for the door. I was still too stunned to say anything, and Kevin was speechless too. Even after he was gone and the door was closed, we both sat there for a second. Why did it feel like he'd robbed of us something after all? I guess he'd taken our dignity.

Finally I said, "What a twit! He's an evil little twit!"

Kevin started laughing—not at me, at the situation. "Jesus," he said. "Talk about cojones."

"No!" I said. "This isn't funny! Before we can laugh about it, you have to admit he's an evil little twit."

"He's an evil little twit," Kevin said, but he didn't stop chuckling.

I turned for the bathroom.

"Oh, hey, can I make a request?" Kevin said.

"Huh?" I said, still pissed off by Daniel (and by Kevin for not being pissed off enough).

"How about we start keeping the seat down when we flush?"

"What?"

"I guess every time you flush the toilet, the water sends all these particles up into the air."

"No way," I said.

"I know, it's disgusting. But if you close the lid, that doesn't happen."

"Not that."

"What?"

"They were all talking about this at the development meeting last week. When did airborne fecal particles become a 'thing'?"

"It's not a 'thing'," Kevin said. "There was an article about it on Salon. But what do you think? Just for number two, not necessarily for number one."

"What I think is that the romance in this relationship is officially dead."

Kevin glared at me.

"Not just dead!" I said. "It's buried and decomposed and now the bones are gone, and even the bacteria that finally ate the bones are dead and have decomposed a couple of times over."

"Russel—"

"Come on, you know I have a point! We're talking airborne fecal particles!'

"*You're* talking airborne fecal particles. I was trying to keep it all nice and vague and euphemistic."

"Admit that the romance in this relationship is dead," I said.

"I'm not going to admit that!" Kevin said, mock-indignant. "The romance in this relationship is alive and kicking. There's so much romance in this relationship that the landlord is going to sue us for violating the terms of our lease, because of the additional occupant."

I stepped closer to him. "Admit the romance in this relationship is dead, and then we can figure out what to do to get it back."

Kevin smirked. "What did you have in mind?"

I slipped my hand into the front of his shorts. His dick was somehow already half-hard. I started unzipping him, even before we'd kissed.

"This is your idea of romance?" he said.

"No, right now, I just want to fuck. But this weekend, how about we go out together and do something nice?"

Later that afternoon, on our way out to pick up some dinner, Kevin and I ran into Gina and Regina on their way into the building.

"Oh, hey," I said to Gina. "Guess what? Turns out there really might be a ghost in our apartment. A screenwriter killed himself back in 1950. I looked it up at the library."

Kevin looked at me, surprised. "You did? When?"

"A few days ago," I said. I hadn't told him I'd stopped at the library, and now I felt kind of stupid I was telling Gina and Regina first, like I'd been trying to keep secrets (which I kinda sorta had been).

"A suicidal screenwriter?" Regina said. "Impossible!"

"I know," I said, laughing. "Who knew?"

"Hey, you guys busy this Saturday?" Regina said.

"Ginny," Gina said.

"*What?*" She looked back at us. "Gina has a show. We can get you on the comp list."

"Really?" I said, looking at Kevin. We had those vague plans to do something romantic, but that was it. Still, I didn't want to speak for him, not after not telling him about the ghost of the dead screenwriter.

"Sure," Kevin said. "Sounds like fun."

"Okay, but there's one condition," Gina said. "I'm not saying you have to laugh at everything I say. But if something is on the bubble, if you think one of my jokes *might* be funny? Please laugh."

"We promise," I said.

Gina's show was at this little comedy club in Santa Monica called Punchlines. I expected it to be small, and it was, but I didn't expect it to be so crowded, with so many tables and people crammed into such a tiny space. Seriously, does Los Angeles not have fire codes or what? You could barely squeeze between the tables, and we ended up, like, three feet from the stage. I could also complain about the insane price of drinks, but I realize that will make me sound like a small town rube, and also someone who complains a lot, which is all true, but it's not something I like to advertise.

The stage was basically one of those wood pallets that a forklift lifts, with a microphone on a stand, all in front of a brick wall. It wasn't even a brick building—they had their own brick backdrop (probably fake), maybe eight feet long. What is it about comedy clubs and the brick backdrop behind the stage? Clearly, it's just one more thing that serves absolutely no purpose whatsoever, but somehow makes everyone feel better, like neckties or the entire British royal family.

We had to sit through four comics before Gina took the stage. They were all guys, and they made a lot of jokes about how small their penises are and how shitty the Los Angeles traffic is. Seriously, if I'd known what a total cliché that was, I wouldn't have mentioned it earlier.

Three of those four comics were bad, and the fourth outright bombed, which was awkward. But no matter how bad they were, each one of them, even the guy who bombed, also had at least one table of friends who had clearly been encouraged to laugh at anything even remotely funny, like Gina had told us to do. It was really obvious which table was there to see who, mostly because the laughter was so phony. I'm no actor, but when it came time to fake-laugh for Gina, I was determined to do it much more convincingly.

When she finally took the stage, I was actually nervous for her. I barely knew Gina, but the four comics before her had to be going home feeling pretty crappy, especially the guy who outright bombed.

I'm a gold-stars-for-everyone kind of guy: I don't want anyone feeling bad, not even shitty comedians who make bad penis jokes.

For a moment, Gina stood at the microphone, glowering at the crowd, like she was seriously put out, but I knew this had to be part of her act.

Laughter rippled across the room. I laughed too.

Gina still didn't say anything, just glared at us harder.

People laughed again, a little nervous.

"*Whaaaat?*" she said at last, completely impatient.

Everyone laughed now. A couple of people whooped it up and applauded, and somehow I realized that Gina had a catch-phrase.

"*Whaaaat?*" she said again. "You think I'm your bitch? Think I'm your little performing monkey? Well, it don't work like that! You want my comedy, you have to *earn* it! You *hear* me? You have to fucking *earn* it!"

People started applauding and hollering. Gina looked assuaged, but just barely.

It was a pretty shrewd way to start the show. It was a comedy bit, true, but she'd also immediately established that *she* was calling the shots, that she was in charge. It wasn't like the four previous comedians, who had all acted desperate, like they had something to prove. Gina had totally turned the tables, making it so the audience had something to prove to her.

"This city is such a piece of shit," Gina said. "But no one who lives here seems to realize it. No matter what you say, they always say the same thing: 'But the weather is so great!' Everything smells like ozone and piss, but people say, 'Yeah, but the weather is so great!' The city's completely corrupt and totally segregated, and they say, 'Can you believe how nice it is outside today? And in *March*!' They built this fucking city in a desert, we've sucked the water table dry, and now we're all totally screwed, but they're, like, 'I'm going to sit around the pool! Oh, and yay, In-N-Out Burger!'"

I laughed. It was funny, especially the little coda about In-N-Out Burger, which people here did seem totally obsessed with.

"Just so you guys know," Gina said, "I'm actually a lesbian, and my girlfriend is here tonight."

Gina motioned to Regina, and a couple of guys made lewd catcalls.

Gina gave the guys the look she'd given the whole crowd at the start of the show. "What the hell was *that* for? You guys do realize that the fact that we're lesbians makes us *less* likely to fuck you, right?"

One of the guys booed, which I gave him total props for. I wouldn't have stood up to the woman on that stage.

Gina was impressed too. "Okay," she said, pointing. "*You* we'll fuck."

She'd read the audience exactly right: it got a good laugh.

"Just so you guys also know," Gina said to the whole room, "I'm not just a lesbian. I'm an *angry* lesbian."

The audience oohed and aahed.

"You know *how* angry I am?" Gina asked.

"No!" someone said. "How angry *are* you?"

"I'm not just angry about the usual things—helicopter parents or people who don't clean up after their dogs. I'm angry about *everything*. I'm angry about hub caps. And crown molding. And pinecones. Oh, man, pinecones make me *livid*! Number two pencils. They! Make! My! Blood! Boil! I hate teabags. And dividing lines in roads. Grrrr! Windex, don't get me started on Windex. Morgan Freeman, he can eat shit. I hate ice machines. Oh, and what's the fucking deal with door knobs?"

The audience was eating all this up. I looked at Kevin. He was laughing too, enjoying the show.

"But you know what makes me the *angriest*?" Gina asked the audience.

"What makes you the angriest?" someone called.

"*Dental floss!* Nah, just kidding, it's actually Fox News."

The audience went nuts. She had an absolutely perfect read on them.

"Let's talk about lesbians for a minute," Gina went on. "There are a lot of stereotypes about us. That we hate men. That we want to cut your balls off. That we're going to fuck your wives and girlfriends." She shrugged, indifferent. "You know what they say: sometimes the stereotypes are true."

I kept laughing along with the rest of the crowd.

Gina went on like this for a good twenty minutes, and she kept pretty much killing it. She'd taken the "angry lesbian" stereotype, and somehow made it both subversive and empowering. At the same time, it didn't feel like "inside" jokes that only a lesbian would understand or find funny. Her angry lesbian was somehow universal.

Finally, up on stage, Gina said to the audience, "Lots of 'comedy insiders' told me that I'd never make it as an out lesbian comic. And appearing in this little shithole of a club with an irrelevant audience like you pretty much proves they were right. I'm Gina Carver, thank you and good night!"

The whole room laughed and cheered and applauded, including me, and I realized I hadn't needed to fake-laugh once the whole set.

# CHAPTER EIGHT

After the show, Gina joined Regina and Kevin and me at our table. I would've expected her to look happy, but she didn't.

"You were great!" Kevin said. "Really great."

"I didn't have to fake-laugh at all," I said with a smile.

"Thanks," she said, but it sounded bittersweet.

"What's wrong?" Regina asked Gina.

"Eddy never showed," Gina said.

"This booking agent was supposed to come," Regina explained to Kevin and me.

"Aw, that sucks," Kevin said.

"You guys wanna get something to eat?" Regina said. "Gina can never eat before a show."

"Sure," Kevin said. "Where to?"

Regina looked at Gina. "Stefano's?"

"Fine, whatever," Gina said, obviously sulking.

"They've got things you can eat."

"Yeah, spaghetti without parmesan."

"Okay, since this has to be all about you, where do *you* want to go?"

"What about RAWvolution?"

"Great if you're a rabbit."

Kevin interrupted. "I think there's a diner just down the street."

Gina invited a couple of people to dinner with us, Rodney and Kyle—two of the other comics from that night. They were both sort of hapless straight guys, one black and one white (neither of them was the guy who outright bombed).

As we were waiting for the waitress to take our order, I said to Gina again, "You really were great." Then I remembered that Rodney and Kyle had gone on that night too, so I added, "You all were."

It sounded completely insincere, even to me. I thought back about how I'd been so certain that my fake-laughter would sound real. Sincerity was harder to fake than I thought.

"S'cuse me," Gina said to a passing waitress. "Can I get a Red Hook?"

"I never realized how much comedy is like writing," I said to the table. "I mean, I know it *is* writing. But what makes a successful comedy set is exactly what makes a successful screenplay. It's all about the voice."

"Yeah," Kyle said, sort of apologetic. "I had a sore throat tonight."

"No," I said, feeling awkward. "I meant the perspective. That kind of voice, you know? All the jokes revolve around a certain point of view. Something new, something authentic. They're not just random jokes."

I was mostly pulling this out of my ass, and was

frankly worried I sounded like a total tosser. But then Regina piped up and said, "Oh, yeah! It really is the same thing as writing a screenplay."

I smiled at her, grateful. "Anyway, you guys all have great voices." Obviously, I really only meant this about Gina, but I said it to Rodney and Kyle too, because I didn't want to be an asshole. I sounded a little more sincere this time, but not by much.

"You really think so?" Rodney said.

"Oh, yeah!" I said, faking it again. "Totally."

"Thanks," he said, almost pathetically grateful.

"Yeah," Gina said. "Finding my voice sure has made a big difference to *my* career."

Gina didn't sound insecure like Rodney. She sounded pissed.

No one said anything for a second.

"Gina's been a little discouraged lately," Regina said.

"Really?" Gina said to her. "What am I, nine?"

"I wasn't—" Regina protested.

"Just drop it, okay?"

Fortunately, the waitress came back right then with Gina's Red Hook and to take the rest of our orders.

After the waitress left, no one said anything for a second.

Then Kevin, smart enough to try changing the subject, said, "So what do guys think of Key and Peele?" These were two comedians who had a TV show that Kevin and I liked a lot, especially their re-occurring "Obama anger translator" bit.

"They're great," Kyle said, and everyone nodded.

We all relaxed a little in our seats. The subject had officially been changed!

"They're sketch comedians," Gina said, sucking down her beer. "That's not stand-up."

We all tensed again. Gina may have killed on stage tonight, but she also had a habit of killing conversations.

"So who do you guys like?" I said. "Comedians, I mean."

"Louis CK is brilliant," Kyle said. "Aziz Ansari."

"Chris Rock," Rodney said. "Affion Crockett."

"What do you guys think of Kathy Griffin?" I said.

"She doesn't tell jokes," Gina said, drinking again. "She tells stories."

*That's the whole point,* I thought. It was a different kind of comedy. She'd written all about it in her autobiography—how, at one of the lowest points in her career, she reinvented herself over and over until she finally found a way to connect with the audience. But I didn't have the nerve to mention any of this to Gina.

"And lately, she tells those fucking boring stories about reality TV stars," Gina said.

"Yeah," I said, trying to find common ground. "It does seem like she's dumbed it down lately. Her act used to be about making fun of the whole idea of 'celebrity'—how self-important it all is. But now it seems like all she wants to do is gossip."

No one said anything.

"Do you guys think about that?" I said. "Trying to, like, make a point with your comedy? Or is the only thing that matters making the audience laugh?"

As soon as I said it, I realized this was a really stupid question. With Gina in such a foul mood because that booking agent didn't show, I should have tried to steer the conversation away from comedy completely.

"I don't think about any of that," Kyle said, unsure. "I just tell jokes."

"Yeah," Rodney said. "You just wanna make people laugh."

It didn't surprise me that neither of them had thought about what I'd said. It was part of the reason why their acts stank (but only part of it). But it was obvious that Gina must have given this some real thought, so I was actually kinda sorta curious to hear what she had to say.

"What difference does it make?" she said. "It's all a fucking crap shoot anyway." She motioned the waitress for another Red Hook.

Kevin, who was reading the situation exactly like I was, asked Rodney and Kyle, "So where do you guys live?"

"Silver Lake-ish," Rodney said.

"North Ridge," Kyle said.

"I used to think that," Gina said, interrupting, already drunk—she'd clearly started drinking at the club. "That it made a difference. That the system fucking worked. That talent matters. That if you worked hard enough, struggled long enough, you'd eventually get your break. But now I know it's just fucking random chance. Shitty comics make it big all the time, and great comics get screwed."

Stupidly, before I could stop myself, I said to Gina, "But you really were good tonight. It's only a matter of time until someone sees that."

Everyone else at the table sort of grunted and half-nodded in agreement.

"What the hell do *you* know about it?" Gina said. She was glaring at me now, a lot like how she'd stared at the audience from the stage. Her nostrils flared. Suddenly I realized that Gina's comedian voice, her stage persona, was even more authentic than I knew: she really *was* an angry lesbian. It's just that she was mostly angry about her career.

And now she was angry with me. It was one thing to have her stare out at the whole audience, especially when you knew it was part of her act. That was funny. It was something else to have that glare directed right at you. This wasn't funny at all. It was all I could do not to crawl under the table with the sticky floor and loose French fries.

*It wasn't just me!* I wanted to say. *Everyone else grunted in agreement!*

"Stop projecting," Regina said, calm and collected. "You're feeling pissy that Eddy didn't show tonight, but why take it out on the rest of us?"

Now Gina turned her Medusa-like gaze on her girlfriend. "Don't you psychoanalyze me! I don't need your fucking analysis!"

"I'm not psychoanalyzing you," Regina said. "I'm *managing* you. Because that's what I *always* do—I come along behind, cleaning up your messes." She mumbled the rest under her breath: "Sort of like the guy who cleans up after the horse in a parade."

It was funny, but no one laughed. I think we were all too scared to inhale. Even Gold Bond Ultimate Comfort Body Powder wasn't keeping me from sweating now, profusely.

"Thanks for the fucking sympathy!" Gina said to Regina. "It's just so fucking easy for you to sit there with your little judgments, and your snide comments. You have no idea what it's like up there, how hard it is!"

"Yes, yes, we already covered all this," Regina said. "You're such a victim. You're *so* incredibly brilliant, and the world just *refuses* to recognize your genius. Delusions of grandeur much?" Now she motioned to the waitress. "I changed my mind. Could I get a Hennessey?"

Gina breathed in, like a dragon inhaling before unleashing a column of fire through its mouth. Kevin, Rodney, Kyle, and I were all looking everywhere except at the two of them. I noticed a small splotch of dried mustard on the wall, yellow and cracked.

What Gina and Regina were doing wasn't gentle teasing, like what Kevin and I did. It was all-out warfare. Somehow I felt responsible. I mean, yes, this was mostly about Gina and Regina, about some weird dynamic they had—some oil and water clash between emotion and logic, and the two of them driving each other crazy. But I'd started this conflict with those stupid questions of mine. Mostly, I just wanted to slither out of that restaurant on my stomach, the way the Grinch crawls around Whoville in *How the Grinch Stole Christmas*. Unfortunately, we'd already ordered and couldn't leave until our food came.

So I interrupted Gina before she could talk. "I have no idea what I'm talking about!" I said quickly. "I mean, I haven't even been in this town two months. What do I know?" I laughed. "God, I'm sure you're right. It's probably all random chance."

I was faking it again, and anyone who was listening could totally hear the insincerity in my voice. But Regina at least saw how uncomfortable they were making us, and maybe even Gina got the hint. The fire temporarily dimmed in her eyes, and the waitress returned with Regina's drink.

I'd thrown myself on the sword, and the tension was momentarily released.

The six of us kept on talking, with Kevin and me trying to keep the topic on things that had nothing whatsoever to do with comedy or even entertainment in general. Gina and Regina sniped, and Gina sulked and stewed, but we managed to make it through the meal without it completely descending into a scene from some depressing HBO sitcom.

At one point, though, I pulled out my phone and sent Kevin a text from under the table:

**Promise me we'll NEVER EVER EVER be like Gina and Regina!!!!!**

Finally, the waitress came and asked the table, "So did you guys leave room for dessert?"

Kevin and I both said, at exactly the same time, "No, we're ready for the check!"

After dinner, Kevin and I said our quick goodbyes, then we went for a walk. It was late—almost midnight—but there was still plenty of life on the Third Avenue Promenade, which is this outdoor shopping mall in downtown Santa Monica. The street's closed off to car traffic, and there are shops and fountains and restaurants and sidewalk cafes and buskers. It's mostly a lot of chains—the Gap, Forever 21, Johnny Rockets—but it's still pretty cool.

"Well, that was unbelievably awkward," Kevin said, meaning dinner with Gina and Regina.

"No kidding," I said.

It *had* been weird, but now that it was over, I was back to feeling pretty good. It was partly the development meeting at Mr. Brander's house earlier in the week (in which I had *ruled*). It was also the idea that I'd written something that people were actually responding to—proof that I had found my own voice, that I really did have something to say to the world, something the world wanted to hear.

Oh, and all those movies about Hollywood, about how people supposedly had to choose between sucess and their soul? They didn't seem to be true at all.

But it was more than that too. I looked around us at the lights and the bustle of people, even this late at night. There was a woman in a dress that could only be described as "sexy apiarist" (including a netted hood-like feature). It wasn't a costume or anything—it looked like she was just out on the town. Another guy was wearing his Nehru jacket inside-out, and I had no idea if he was being ironic, or if maybe he'd spilled something on himself at dinner.

It was funny. Back in Seattle, I couldn't have cared less about fashion, about haircuts and clothing. I was barely even aware of it (as Otto had pointed out). But now I was: for the first time in my life, I was cognizant of *shoes*. Kevin and I were living in Los Angeles, the cultural center of the whole country, the place where trends *began*. Two years from now, the rest of the country would be imitating the city around me, their shoes and haircuts and clothing—from Daniel's stupid pulled-out pockets to maybe even "sexy apiarist" (who the hell knows?).

I could make a difference too. That's why it excited me, being in the center of all this. I wasn't going to make my mark on the fashion world (not by a long shot), but maybe I could change the culture when it came to my screenplays—when it came to my *ideas*.

I was twenty-four years old, and for the first time in my life, I felt like an adult. Like I mattered.

"Oh! See that?" I said, pointing to a crêpe place on one of the street corners on the Third Street Promenade. "That used be to the record store where Molly Ringwald meets Andrew McCarthy in *Pretty in Pink*."

"Ah," Kevin said.

"You don't sound very impressed."

"Well, I mean, *Pretty in Pink*."

"Yeah, Blane was no Jake Ryan, was he?" Blane was Molly Ringwald's love interest in *Pretty in Pink*, and he was incredibly boring. Jack Ryan was Molly Ringwald's love interest in *16 Candles*, and he was incredibly boring too, but also very, very hot. "Besides," I went on, "Duckie was so obviously gay, but the movie didn't have the guts to go there."

"I've always been more of a *Breakfast Club* kind of guy," Kevin said.

"Oh, me too!" I said. I stopped and did my best Ally-Sheedy-in-*The-Breakfast-Club* impression. "'When you grow up, your heart dies.'"

"'We're all pretty bizarre,'" Kevin said, quoting Emilio Estevez. "'Some of us are just better at hiding it.'"

Together, we laughed. But Kevin wasn't laughing as much as I was—it was more of a loose smile.

"What is it?" I said.

"It's all good," he said. "Hey, you wanna split a bag of kettle corn?"

Santa Monica is located near the beach, so we eventually made our way over to Palisades Park, which is this walkway at the top of a bluff looking out over the water. From there, you can see the Pacific Ocean, and also down to the Santa Monica Pier, which is one of those old-fashioned amusement parks with rides and carnival games and food stands that sells hot dogs and cotton candy.

The night was warm, but the breeze off the water was cool and soothing. It smelled like the ocean, and the eucalyptus trees in the park, and popcorn from the pier.

It was incredibly romantic, and Kevin and I had said before that we were going to have a romantic night out.

So why didn't it *feel* romantic? Was the romance really dead in our relationship? I'd thought that had been a joke.

"That's where they filmed a bunch of movies," I said, prattling on, pointing down to the pier. "*Forrest Gump, The Sting, Ruthless People.*"

Kevin didn't say anything.

"*Hannah Montana: The Movie,*" I said.

He looked at me and smiled. "Sorry," he said. "I'm being a dud."

"What's up?"

He stepped to the guard railing and looked out over the bluff. "I don't know."

"You're still thinking about dinner," I said, "aren't you?"

"Sort of."

"I wonder what that was all about. I mean, it was Gina, yeah. But it was Regina too—the two of them together. I can't imagine our being like that."

"We wouldn't," Kevin said. "We'd break up if we ever treated each other like that."

This was true. Like I said before, Kevin doesn't put up with shit. But it was still weird, hearing him say this out loud.

"Well, there you go," I said.

"But that's not even what's bugging me," he said. "It's not about them, it's about this city. There's something wrong here. You can feel it."

"What do you feel?"

He thought for a second. "The desperation." He turned to look at me. "You know? It's all around us. You can feel it in everyone we meet. You can taste it in the air, like salt off the ocean."

Part of me wanted to go back to quoting John Hughes movies.

Kevin had surprised me. This wasn't what I'd been feeling at all. But I knew what he was saying. It was the dark side to this city, the opposite of everything I'd been thinking before. I thought about all the people I'd met so far—Gina, Regina, Otto, Kyle, Rodney, even Mr. Brander and the other producers. They all desperately wanted something: namely, success in an industry where success was insanely elusive. The entertainment industry really wasn't like other professions. It was so much more competitive. If you go to med school or law school, you usually end up a doctor or a lawyer. Maybe not everyone, but most people, at least if you finish.

But in the entertainment industry, most people *don't* make it. There's even a famous statistic among screenwriters: given all the screenplays that get registered every year with the Writers Guild of America, you actually have a better chance of winning the California State Lottery than you do of selling your screenplay to a movie studio. And even if Gina was being a big bulging Hefty bag of negativity at dinner tonight, she wasn't entirely wrong: luck probably *did* play some role in who ended up making it and who didn't. What was weird was that Kevin hadn't even talked to most of the people I had, and he'd picked up on all this anyway. I guess he was meeting the same kinds of people I was through his job with IMDb, having the same kinds of sad conversations.

"I think the desperation is just part of the city," I said. "Like palm trees and taco trucks. The stakes are high, because this is the big time. People are pursuing their dreams. Make it or break it. Isn't that a good thing? Isn't it like, I don't know...the Olympics?"

"It seems like it broke Gina and Regina," Kevin said.

"That's not the city," I said. "That's them."

"Is it?"

"Kevin, I'm serious. Los Angeles isn't going to break us. You don't need to worry about that."

He didn't say anything, just kept staring out at the water. The neon lights on the rides of the pier down below us flashed on his face—green and red and blue and yellow.

I felt guilty. This move to Los Angeles had been *my* idea. I was the one pursuing *my* dream. Kevin was basically here to support me. Now it sounded like he was regretting it.

"Kevin?"

He looked me. "What happens if you don't make it?"

"What?" I didn't like the turn this conversation was taking. I immediately thought of Cole Gordon, how he'd killed himself in our apartment because he hadn't been able to sell a screenplay (or so I'd decided). An image of the paramedics carrying him out of our apartment on a stretcher flashed through my mind.

"What if it doesn't happen for you?" Kevin said.

"But it will. It *is*. Things are going great."

"I know. And I'm sure everything's going to be great with *A Cup of Joe*. But what if, for some reason, it isn't? What if—I don't know—Mr. Brander dies tomorrow?"

I hadn't really thought about that. Given Mr. Brander's age, it wasn't impossible. But it still irritated me, Kevin bringing it up like this.

"So I'll make a deal with someone else," I said with a shrug. "I mean, it's a good script—all the other producers said so. It's my fourth screenplay, and it was good enough to get optioned. And Fiona's going to represent me."

"You heard back from her?"

"No, not yet." The truth is, I was still too scared to email her and ask what she thought of my screenplays. "But I'm sure she will. I mean, I just made her fifteen hundred dollars."

"You got the check from Mr. Brander?"

"Well, no, I haven't got that yet either." I'd gone from being irritated with Kevin to outright annoyed by him. "But I'm sure we will, any day now. And, I mean, if I don't, if it all falls through, and if I can't find anyone to take this script, I'll write another one. And another one after that. I mean, I'm talented, right?"

"Gina is talented."

This hit me a little bit like a punch. Yes, luck played a part in making it in Hollywood, but only a small part, or at least that's what I told myself. So how did I explain Gina? She was talented—really, really talented. And yet here she was in her forties, still playing shitty little comedy clubs. It hadn't happened for her. So maybe she was more right at dinner than I knew.

The voice in our apartment that night had said, *Whatever you do, don't—* It had felt like a warning, like something bad was about to happen, but what had been the second part of the warning? *Don't ever give your up dream? Don't listen to the nay-sayers?*

"Why are you doing this?" I said to Kevin. "Are you trying to get me to doubt myself?"

"Oh, God, no!" Kevin stepped closer, taking me in his arms. "I'm sorry. That was so stupid. I don't know why I said all that. Forgive me, okay?" He was like one of those mimes that adjust their face with a swipe of their hand: freaked out one second, happy the second.

He kissed me. I could taste the sweetness of kettle corn on his breath, and also the bitterness of the coffee he'd had at dinner.

"Forget I said all that," he said. "We came here to have a romantic night, so let's have one, okay?"

I stared at him for a second. Then I changed my face too, all in an instant, like another mime. I nodded and said, "Yeah. Definitely. One romantic night—order up!"

Kevin laughed.

We turned and walked on through the park, holding hands and once again talking about everything except the entertainment industry. From time to time, we stopped and looked out over the water, and eventually we ended up down at the Santa Monica Pier, where we shared a funnel cake and laughed and rode the Pacific Wheel.

It looked romantic, like in a movie, but it wasn't. I could tell Kevin was distracted. He could probably sense something in me too, the fact that I was still annoyed with him for the things he'd said, the seeds of doubt he'd sewn.

Like I said before, sincerity is a lot harder to fake than you think.

# CHAPTER NINE

That Wednesday afternoon, Mr. Brander and Lewis had arranged a reading of *A Cup of Joe* in a little theater on Melrose. It was just for the producers and me, to hear how the screenplay sounded out loud.

I'd been nervous about the development meeting the week before, but I wasn't (that) nervous about this, mostly because that first meeting had gone so well. I'd killed then, and I was almost certain I was going to kill again today.

But that was before things started to go wrong.

Traffic was horrible (and the Earth was round, and water was wet), and almost the only street parking for miles around was one or two-hour (which I knew wouldn't be enough), so I was late. When I finally found the theater, I was sweaty and out of breath.

There was a small lobby inside. The air was musty, like the furniture section in a Goodwill store. There was a table by the door covered with stacks of glossy postcards, mostly askew—advertisements for other little fringe theaters that probably only survived by casting their shows with lots of actors and then having them guilt their friends into buying tickets.

I heard voices: Mr. Brander and Lewis and Bryce conferring over by the concessions stand (four dollar Pepsis—no doubt the second big source of revenue for a little theater like this). It was strange to think of Mr. Brander being anywhere other than that old house of his. Even in his wheelchair, it felt like an ancient redwood tree had somehow pulled up its roots and wandered out of the forest.

"Yeah, but I told you this at the start," Bryce was saying to Mr. Brander. "I passed up another job for this, and I had a very specific set of conditions." He sounded upset.

"Now calm down, my boy," Mr. Brander said. "We can work this out. It was just a small misunderstanding."

*What's this?* I thought. *Some kind of argument?*

Lewis intercepted me halfway across the lobby. "You're here," he said.

"Yeah," I said. "Sorry I'm late."

"I should've warned you about the parking. There's a long-term lot, but it's hard to find."

I was looking at Lewis, and nodding, but I was trying to hear what Bryce and Mr. Brander were saying. I couldn't make it out. I did hear Bryce say, "jerking me around," and I also heard Mr. Brander say, "important to trust me."

"Bottled water?" Lewis said, handing me one.

"Uh, sure." I took it. "Everything okay?" I said to Lewis, meaning Bryce and Mr. Brander.

"Yeah, that's nothing," Lewis said, immediately turning toward the thick velvet curtain that covered the door into the theater. "Here, let's have you join everyone else."

Truthfully, I would have preferred to stay and eavesdrop a little longer, but I let him lead me into the theater itself (the curtain was so thick that I could no longer hear Mr. Brander and Bryce).

It was even smaller than I expected, about thirty seats total, on homemade wooden risers on either side of a central aisle. The seats looked down onto the floor of the room, which doubled as the stage. The backdrops were cheap wooden cut-outs painted to look like a living room. They hadn't even bothered to hang real art—they'd just painted pictures and frames onto the wood.

I passed Andrea and Justin, sitting in a couple of the seats on one side.

"Oh," I said. "Hey."

"Hey there!" Andrea said, grinning. "Nervous?"

I smiled back. "Not really," I said, except that wasn't quite true anymore. After overhearing Bryce and Mr. Brander in the lobby, I *was* nervous again. Plus, it occurred to me that I'd never actually heard my screenplay out loud, something that all the screenplay websites say is a *huge* rookie mistake. I hadn't even read it aloud to myself when I was writing it.

Down on the "stage," Evan and a group of actors were milling around, arranging folding chairs, copies of my screenplay in hand. Lewis had said on the phone that the movie still hadn't been cast or anything—these were just actors who were doing Evan a favor, in hopes that the producers might see them in the role and decide, "Yes! We must have you!" But it's not like any of them were recognizable celebrities or anything.

I was still hot after all that driving and running, so I cracked open the bottled water Lewis had given me and started drinking. I walked closer to the stage. Being actors, they were all pretty attractive, like Otto had said. It was obvious who was playing Joe and Milo, because they were the hottest actors of all. In fact, they were so hot that I was way too intimidated to talk to them. Instead, I walked up to an older women in a long scarf (a requirement, apparently, for female actors), who I assumed was playing the grand-mother.

"Hey there," I said. "I'm Russel, the writer?"

Evan heard me and turned around. "Hey!" He turned to the actors. "Everyone? This is Russel, the screenwriter of *A Cup of Joe.*"

The actors all gathered around to tell me how much they loved my script. This included the actors playing Joe and Milo, who were even more insanely handsome close up (I approached them to shake their hands, but technically they were still unapproachable). Once again I knew all these compliments were mostly insincere hot air, and once again I was reminded how even insincere hot air is still a thousand times better than constant rejection.

After a bit, everyone else sort of turned back to their own little clusters, and the older woman I'd introduced myself to before said, "I'm Kate." It was good comic timing, like I'd talked to her, and she'd had to wait all this time before she could respond.

I laughed. "Thanks for doing this," I said to her. "I really appreciate it."

"Oh, sure. And they're right, you know. It really is a good script. I read so much shit. But this is special. I really hope it gets made."

I knew she was probably sucking up to me too. Who knows? When it came to casting, maybe even the lowly screenwriter's opinion could tip the scales. But Kate's compliment did feel more sincere.

"Thanks," I said. Overhearing that argument in the lobby had made me anxious, but talking to Kate had made me feel better again. "So what about you? What are you working on?"

"Hmmm, I'm about to play Joseph Gordon-Levitt's mother," she said. "And I'm up for the queen in Disney's new live-action *Little Mermaid*."

*The Bullshit Factor*, I thought. So what did that really mean? She'd merely auditioned for the Gordon-Levitt film, and *The Little Mermaid* wasn't a feature, but something for the Disney Channel? But I couldn't hold it against her. Otto had said everyone did it, that it was expected.

From behind us in the theater, I heard Mr. Brander say, "Okay, everyone, let's get started, shall we?"

He and Lewis had entered, but Bryce was right behind him, his fists clenched. "I'll walk!" he said to Mr. Brander. "I'm serious! This is bullshit and you know it. I'll walk out of this theater right now, and I won't be back."

With a spine as straight as the redwood tree I mentioned earlier, Mr. Brander stared straight ahead. "By all means, do what you have to do."

As Bryce stood there staring daggers down at Mr. Brander's wheelchair, an awkward silence descended on the room. I saw Andrea and Justin glance at each other, the way people do when they're quietly mortified by right-wing grandparents. Lewis looked at his shoes.

*Not in front of the actors,* I thought, as if they were children.

Finally, Bryce laughed. "You're crazy," he said. "You're a crazy old man! This is such bullshit. Okay, I'm gone!"

It took more than one try for Bryce to find the actual opening in the velvet curtain behind him, but then he fumbled his way through and disappeared.

Mr. Brander rolled forward down the aisle. Out in the lobby, the door slammed loud enough to be heard even through the curtain.

*What in the world was* that *about?* I thought. Was Bryce gone for good, and if so, what did it mean for our movie? But I wasn't about to ask. I didn't even move a muscle for fear that Mr. Brander would notice me and make a big deal about my presence like he usually did. Instead, he started to direct the actors on who should sit where.

"Okay, where's Joe?" Mr. Brander said.

"Ross?" Evan said, and one of the actors stepped forward.

"What?" Mr. Brander said.

"I'm Joe," the actor said.

"Who's Ross?" Mr. Brander said.

"I am," the actor said. "I'm playing Joe."

"Oh! Right." He pointed to a chair. "You're there. And Milo?"

"Nicholas?" Evan said, nodding to another actor. "And Marcy is Megan."

Mr. Brander hesitated, clearly confused by all the different names. He looked at Evan. "Why don't we stick to character names for now, okay?"

"Okay," Evan said. "Sorry."

And so Mr. Brander went down the line arranging

the actors, but I could tell that Evan, Andrea, and Justin were a little concerned by how easily Mr. Brander had become confused. Plus, everyone was probably still wondering about what had happened with Bryce. Meanwhile, Lewis busied himself by passing out more bottled waters. Basically, there were whole layers of subtext to this room that Mr. Brander seemed completely unaware of, or was maybe choosing to ignore.

*He's probably still flustered by his argument with Bryce*, I thought. *I would be.*

"Okay," Mr. Brander said to the group. "I realize none of you have read the script."

From one side, Evan spoke up. "They've read the script."

Mr. Brander looked at him, confused again.

"They've read the script," he repeated. "Most of them anyway. They haven't had any rehearsal, but they read the script. And I'll be reading the scene descriptions."

Mr. Brander still looked a little befuddled. "That's fine," he said quietly.

To the actors, Evan said, "We're not looking for perfection. We just want to go all the way through, out loud, so all of us, and Russel here, can hear how it sounds."

At the sound of my name, Mr. Brander finally perked up again. He searched for me in the seats. "Russel! How are you, my boy?" Now he sounded like he always did, completely confident, owning the room.

I squeezed out a smile. "I'm good. Thanks, Mr. Brander."

After that, the actors started in on the script. I was

still a bit freaked out by everything that had happened, plus I was sitting in a theater where my words were being performed in front of me for the very first time in my life.

So basically, I didn't hear a single word that the actors said.

Then ten minutes into the reading, something even worse happened: I realized I had to pee. It had been a long drive over, and also a long time searching for parking, then I'd quickly guzzled down that whole bottled water that Lewis had given me. Stupidly, it hadn't occurred to me to go to the bathroom before the reading. By the time we were twenty minutes into the script, I *really* had to go. I was also realizing there probably wouldn't be an intermission (after all, it was the script of a *movie*, not a play, with no natural stopping point).

At least I was on the aisle. I was pretty sure I could slip out without being too disruptive. Granted, this was a reading of *my* screenplay, and a big part of why we were here was so I could hear the damn thing out loud, but I wasn't listening anyway. Yes, everyone in the theater would definitely see me leave, but what alternative did I have?

Then I thought back to that little lobby behind me. I didn't remember there being any doors to restrooms—and it was small enough that if there *had* been doors, I would've seen them. The only other door in the whole theater other than the entrance seemed to be the door in the stage itself, to backstage.

*The only restrooms in this theater are backstage?* I thought. What was I going to do, get up, walk through the actors on stage, then wander around back there looking for the bathroom?

*Oh, blimey,* I thought. I'd never used, or even thought, the words "Oh, blimey" in my life, but I thought them right then.

This was too embarrassing, even for me. It didn't seem like I could possibly hold it for another sixty minutes. On the other hand, disrupting the reading would have been completely mortifying, so I didn't have any choice.

I like to think the stuff I write reads at a relatively brisk pace, that I include conflict in every scene and never forget my narrative arcs.

But sitting in that theater with my bladder threatening to burst like an appendix, my screenplay dragged something crazy. If people in Los Angeles wore jackets, I would have seriously considered putting mine over my lap and trying to pee into the empty water bottle.

Finally—FINALLY!—my endless, wildly-overwritten, hopelessly meandering screenplay came to an end.

"Thanks so much," Evan was saying to the actors. "You were all just great."

Andrea turned around to me in the seats. "You okay with us sharing our notes now?"

"Absolutely," I said, standing and pretending to stretch. "But how about a five-minute break? Not that the screenwriter desperately needs to pee or anything!"

This got a laugh from everyone who heard me, including Mr. Brander, and I was back to thinking: *I can do this! I can be funny and charming when I need to be.*

By the time I got back from the restroom, the actors had all left, and the producers had moved into the seats along the front of the stage. Mr. Brander's wheelchair was in the aisle, so I settled into one of the folding chairs on stage, with me in the hot seat. Now we were just waiting on Lewis who had been using the restroom after me.

Nobody was saying anything. I'd sat down into the middle of an awkward silence. Evan, Justin, and Andrea all eyed each other, unsettled.

*Now what?* In a way, it had been a good thing I desperately had to use the bathroom all through the reading, because it meant I was too preoccupied to obsess about everything that had happened before—Bryce storming out and the general obtuseness of Mr. Brander. But I was funny and charming, right? Somehow I'd figure out a way to make this right, to make everyone feel okay about this damn movie project again.

Sitting his wheelchair, Mr. Brander began to snore. It was very quiet, but impossible to ignore, since nobody else was saying anything. At some point in the last few minutes, he'd fallen asleep. That's what was causing the awkwardness. So much for his being a noble old redwood tree.

Lewis appeared at last, coming up next to Mr. Brander's wheelchair and tapping him on the shoulder.

"Mr. Brander?" he said, and the old man jerked awake.

But the damage was long since done. I could see it on Andrew, Justin, and Evan's faces—a cross between laughing at Mr. Brander and freaking out as they realized what kind of pathetic geriatric they'd partnered with on this film. Basically, there was more subtext on the stage right then than in any play that little theater had probably ever put on.

*Are they going to leave?* I thought. *Throw down their scripts and storm out of the theater like Bryce?* Well, why not? If Mr. Brander was a joke, what was the point of staying? I guess Kevin had been right that night in Santa Monica when he said the movie deal would fall apart. If I had any self-respect, I'd leave too. The problem was, I didn't have anywhere else to go. No other producers wanted me.

"Well, that was just great!" I said to the group. "The reading was just *so, so* helpful to me." Who knows? If I hadn't been so distracted, maybe it really would've been.

"Hmm?" Mr. Brander said, still groggy from his afternoon nap.

"But mostly I want to hear what *you* folks thought," I said, quickly moving on, ignoring Mr. Brander and concentrating on Evan, Andrea, and Justin. "What do you guys think didn't work about the script? Of course"—at this I cleared my throat mock-modestly—"you can also tell me what you thought *worked.*"

Everyone laughed. The ominous subtext from before was gone, for the moment at least. I could see that in their eyes too.

They did tell me what they liked about *A Cup of Joe* (he said modestly). They also told me what they thought was wrong. Scenes that dragged and needed to be tightened, lines that didn't work or were confusing, stuff like that.

I agreed with some of it and thought some of it was stupid, but I nodded and wrote it all down on my iPad. Mostly I was just glad that the discussion was keeping the other producers distracted from Mr. Brander.

"The problem is the present-day storyline."

Mr. Brander had spoken at last.

The other producers and I all turned to look at him, sitting tall and straight in his wheelchair again. The fog had lifted from his eyes.

"We all agree that the flashbacks are terrific," he went on, suddenly as confident and solid as, well, a redwood tree. "Smart and funny and brisk and surprising. In fact, they're so good they disguise the fact that nothing happens in the present-day storyline. Joe and Milo meet, and they have a series of conversations, some of which are quite witty. But what *happens*? Yes, Milo has a new boyfriend, but they're clearly not in love. So where are the *obstacles* to him and Joe getting together? All the real action is in the past, so it's really just a question of the two of them realizing they should be together, that they never should have broken up in the first place. But where's the dramatic tension in that? It's almost all internal. If this was a novel, we might be able to get away with that, but it's not, it's a movie. So we need more. Let's make *this* cup of joe much, much hotter. Scalding!"

No one said a word. We all just stared.

"Milo needs to be more in love with his new boyfriend?" I said.

"*At least!*" Mr. Brander said. "Give him a live-in boyfriend, a mother with Alzheimer's, terminal cancer, and an internship in Paris! Let's make it *insanely* difficult for these two boys to get together!" His eyes twinkled. "Okay, maybe not, but you know what I mean. The point is, the harder they have to fight to get back together, the more obstacles they have to overcome, then the more the audience will love us when they finally *do*."

We all sat there, sort of in awe of everything he'd just said. Behind the wheelchair, Lewis suppressed a smile.

Mr. Brander was absolutely right about my screenplay, and we all knew it—me, the stupid screenwriter who had written the whole damn thing and never seen that incredibly glaring flaw, and the other producers, who had spent the last twenty minutes discussing it, but who hadn't said anything close to what Mr. Brander had said, despite it being the script's most obvious weakness.

In short, Mr. Brander was reminding us that he may have been older than the hydrogen atom—he may have gotten confused by too many names and sometimes even fell asleep in readings—but he still knew something about making movies.

I looked from Andrea to Justin to Evan, and it was like I could literally see the doubt leaving their eyes like little butterflies fluttering off into the distance. My plan had worked! I'd distracted the producers long enough for Mr. Brander to finally reassure them that he knew what the hell he was doing on this little movie of ours.

But the reality was, I'd been starting to wonder again about Mr. Brander myself. So the other good part of all this was that the butterflies of doubt were fluttering away from me too.

Truthfully, I didn't really want to go home that night. Kevin was going to ask me about the reading, and I didn't want to lie to him, but I didn't want to tell him the truth either. I could just say, "It went great!" and leave it at that, because it *had* been pretty great in the end. But we weren't that kind of couple. We didn't keep secrets (except dumb little ones, like secret cookie-binging and the occasional online cyber-scx romp). But if I told him everything that had really happened, I knew he'd jump to all the wrong conclusions. The point is, I didn't want to have a fight about his negativity about the movie project, not now when I was actually back to feeling pretty good about things.

Anyway, when I got back to the apartment building, I saw Regina and Zoe, Daniel's sister, sitting in the courtyard next to the pool. Regina was stretched out in one of the lounge chairs with a screenplay on her lap, and Zoe looked like she'd stopped to chat on her way in from work. So Zoe had a problem with Kevin and me being gay, but not Gina and Regina? That didn't seem fair.

Even so, I stopped. There was no point in my not being polite.

"Hey, there," I said.

They both looked over at me. They had different expressions: Regina looked flustered and Zoe's face darkened. The point is, neither one looked particularly happy to see me. Maybe I'd interrupted something between them.

Regina's mouth quickly segued into a friendly smile, but Zoe's didn't.

"Russel!" Regina said. "What's up? Have a seat—join us."

Now I didn't know what to do. Did they really want me to join them? On the other hand, I was still dreading seeing Kevin, so I sat down, but I felt stiff and out of place.

"Where you coming from?" Regina asked.

I told them about the *A Cup of Joe* reading, and also (briefly) that weird conversation I'd had with Kevin over the movie project before, and now how I didn't know what to say to him about how it went.

"Lie," Regina said.

"Really?" I said.

She nodded. "Maybe he'll understand, but maybe he won't, and it's not worth the hassle."

I considered this, but then immediately thought: *Should I really be taking relationship advice from Regina?*

I looked at Zoe, implicitly asking her opinion.

"Oh, who the hell knows?" she said. "Tell him, or don't. What difference does it make?" I know this sounds like she was blowing me off, but it came out more like she was frustrated with her own life. Knowing Daniel, it was probably frustration with him.

"How'd you end up living with your brother anyway?" I said, but then immediately regretted it. I'd sort of spoken without thinking. What if their parents had died? What if she didn't like me assuming she'd been talking about Daniel when she'd been so frustrated just then?

Her eyes latched onto me. There was still suspicion in them, but there was something else too: respect? She was impressed I'd figured out what had frustrated her. She didn't know that subtext happened to be my specialty, especially lately.

"Our parents were deported," she said. "More than ten years ago now."

"Oh, man, that so sucks," I said.

"But Daniel and I were both born here."

"So they're U.S. citizens," Regina said, and I nodded. It was interesting how Zoe didn't have the slightest trace of a Mexican accent, but Daniel did, even though it sounded like he'd spent his whole life in the U.S. What was that about?

"Anyway," Zoe went on, "Daniel was just a kid, but I was twenty-two, so we all decided that he and I would stay here, and I'd more or less raise him."

"That's a lot of pressure," I said, commiserating, and Zoe nodded. There was also an implied "but" in there somewhere, but for once I didn't want to be the one to bring it up.

"We had a plan," Zoe said. "I'd get a job, and Daniel would go to school."

*But Daniel hasn't lived up to his part of the bargain*, I thought. *Or if he has, he's done the bare minimum.*

"I've almost got him through high school," Zoe said. "Then I need to get him through college."

*Daniel in college?* I thought. *Not hardly.* But I immediately felt guilty for thinking it.

"Well, Kevin and I said we'd help him with his homework," I said.

Zoe's face instantly darkened again. "When?"

"When he was in our apartment."

"In your apartment?" Her face got darker still. She wasn't quite scowling, but it was close. I guess I'd known that Zoe didn't like Kevin and me, and I'd even known the reason why: Daniel had basically told us she thought her two gay neighbors were going to hit on her teenage brother. This wasn't even subtext anymore—it was outright text.

"It was last week," I said, feeling guilty again, but not quite sure what for. "He came to us. He knocked on our door."

She held up her hands, sort of a surrender. "I'm sorry. It's just..."

"He's driving you crazy," Regina said.

Zoe nodded. "I've worked so hard. And it feels like..."

"He's throwing it all away."

She nodded again, tightly.

I looked down at Zoe's hands, now clasped together on her lap. The knuckles were white, and the fingers were rough and blistered, skin flaking. I still didn't know what Zoe did for a living—I'd assumed she worked in an office, but who knows? Maybe she was a nurse, or a teacher who cleaned up after small kids. Anyway, she was literally working her hands to the bone for Daniel, and he was too stupid to appreciate it.

Some part of me felt like I should be mad at Zoe for basically implying that Kevin and I were molesting her brother—or even *interested* in molesting her brother. But I wasn't mad, or even offended. In fact, she was breaking my heart. Zoe and I didn't seem to have much in common, but we both desperately wanted something: she wanted a future for her little brother, and I wanted my damn screenplay to be turned into a movie—proof that I wasn't a fuck up, that I had something to say to the world, something the world wanted to hear.

I was about to say something sympathetic when Kevin appeared in the courtyard.

"Oh!" I said. "Hey."

"Hey," he said, barely glancing over.

"Where were you?"

"Out for a walk." His shoulders were clenched, and he didn't move closer toward us, so I figured he wasn't in the mood to be social.

I looked at Regina and Zoe, sort of excusing myself with my eyes, then headed over Kevin's way.

As we walked up the stairs to our apartment, I said, "What's going on?"

"Charles is an *asshole*, that's what's going on!" Charles was one of Kevin's supervisors. This wasn't the first time Kevin had complained about him.

"Why? What did he do?"

"You know, I don't even care that he's so eager to dumb the site down. What else is new? What I *don't* get is why he's not worried that everyone is going to see us as just another corporate shill. Credibility is the one thing we offer that other sites don't have. It's our whole fucking *brand*!"

We were inside the apartment now, so I said, "What does he want you to do?"

Kevin went off. (And in fairness to Kevin, it really did sound like Charles was being even more of an asshole than usual.)

But as Kevin talked, it occurred to me that he was so distracted by Charles that he wasn't going to ask me how the reading had gone. So I didn't have to make the choice between telling him what had happened or lying like Regina had said. I mean, Kevin already had a lot on his mind. Why add to it?

Look, I'm not arguing that I deserve credit for this or anything, that I was being particularly noble. Still, at the time, it seemed like a perfectly reasonable thing to do.

# CHAPTER TEN

That Saturday, Otto invited me over to his place in Fairfax for another reading, this time of the scripts for the first season of his web series.

He lived in a big old house with a bunch of friends. It had seven bedrooms, I think, with at least ten people living there. They were all artists of some kind: actors, writers, filmmakers, and musicians. I guess you could say it was sort of a collective, that by living together as a group, they could all somehow manage to get by. According to Otto, there was always someone rehearsing a play or a music gig. They called their house the Hive—there was even a sign over the front door with painted bees and everything—which I thought was cool.

One thing I noticed right away: they weren't the cleanest bunch in the world. Actually, the place was disgusting. I seriously wondered if it had ever been vacuumed since the first Hivers had moved in however many years ago. There was the layer of grime you could see, like the dirt on the floor and Doritos crumbs on the couch, but then there was another layer you couldn't quite see, a stickiness to the lino-leum and a feeling of general ickiness on all the furniture, like the vague fuzz on cheese that's gone bad. Not surprisingly, the house smelled like the alley behind a tavern. Oh, and there was equipment every-where—cameras, guitars and amps, computers—but the tables and countertops were also covered with half-filled beer bottles and empty pizza boxes.

By this point, I had totally accepted that I needed to make sacrifices for my own art—packing up and moving to traffic-choked Los Angeles, spending too much money on a crappy one-bedroom apartment that didn't even have a working oven. But having to sit on that disgusting toilet in the Hive bathroom? Sorry, that would be beyond me.

There were eight people to read Otto's scripts. Everyone had a part, but it was the real actors who had the actual roles. (I was reading a bunch of char-acters who only had one line each: Barista, Producer #3, Receptionist, Spectator #2, and Parking Lot Attendant.)

Otto introduced me around, and I kinda sorta wanted him to say, "This is the guy with the movie in development," but he didn't.

Sadly, it was immediately clear who was an actor, and who was a writer or other artist. Basically, the actors were all hot, sometimes shockingly so, and the writers and musicians weren't, also sometimes shock-ingly so. I was starting to see Otto's point about the Screenwriter Loophole. (There were also other divi-sions, like the fact that the musicians were completely covered with tattoos and piercings, and the actors and writers were mostly clean-cut, but this went beyond the scope of Otto's Hollywood tutorial.)

I talked to one guy, Jon (a hot actor), asking him where I might have seen him.

"Well," he said, "on Tumblr, someone pasted Darren Criss' face onto some nude modeling shots I did a few years back."

I smiled, even as I made a mental note to try to find those photos when I got home.

I talked to Lionel (a not-so-hot screenwriter), who told me about a new program where if you made less than twice the poverty level in Los Angeles—twenty-two thousand dollars a year—you could get a card that let you ride mass transit for half price.

And I talked to Maisy (another hot actor), who told me she'd gone to an audition the week before, and she'd been halfway through her reading when she'd realized that neither of the "producers" were wearing pants. (They'd actually wanted her to sign a release so they could post it to some fetish website.)

At this point, I thought, *Wait a minute, what about the Bullshit Factor?* None of Otto's friends were trying to impress me with wildly-inflated credits. On the contrary, they were telling me the actual truth about their lives as artists: how much they were struggling, how humiliating it could be. I guess it was because these were all Otto's friends, or maybe because it was just a web series reading, and the stakes were so much lower. Either way, I liked it. I never did bring up *A Cup of Joe*, and I was glad I hadn't.

Finally, we gathered to read through the scripts (and I quickly excused myself to use the bathroom one last time, despite the fact that it was so very disgusting). When I got back, Otto said to the group, "Before we start, I wanted to say thanks to my friend

Russel, who gave me the idea for this web series in the first place."

"I did not," I said, totally blushing. "You thought of it." But I was flattered he'd given me the nod.

We read the scripts after that. Each episode was only about five minutes long, and there were five episodes in all. They were really good, and I'm not just saying that. The first episode introduced the main character: a guy named Otto Digmore who's trying to make it as an actor in Los Angeles, but who also happens to have a big scar on his face.

One of the reoccurring bits of the series was that absolutely every person he meets is totally obsessed with his scar. They stare, they gawk, and they always end up saying, "Does it hurt?" At the end of the first episode, Otto sees a guy on his bike get run over by a car, and he's lying bloody in the middle of the street, dying, and Otto goes over to help him, and the first thing the guy says to Otto is, "Does it hurt?"

This made me feel a little guilty, because when we'd met for lunch that first time, I'd been preoccupied with Otto's scar too. On the other hand, I loved how the whole show was from *Otto's* point of view—how the joke was always on the people who stared and said stupid things, not on him. It never explained how Otto got his scars either, or told you how a person "should" react. It just showed you the reality of his life and let you draw your own conclusions.

There was another reoccurring bit where Otto goes to acting auditions. The producers are always as obsessed with his scar as everyone else, but when the audition is over, and he asks them if he got the part, they always say no, but they never give an honest answer why. Instead, they say things like, "I'm so sorry, we're looking for someone with, uh, fewer arm freckles."

Finally, in the last episode of the season, Otto goes to an audition and gets rejected as usual ("We're looking for someone with, uh, thicker earlobes"). But then Otto confronts the producers, like in the story he told me that day over lunch. And they tell him all the things Otto told me those real-life producers had really said.

Afterward, Otto walks down the street, depressed. In a voice-over, he thoughtfully explains how he can see the producers' point, that his scars *are* distracting, and it's not fair to expect them to risk their careers for *his* issue.

At this point, someone stops him on the street and says, "Does it hurt?"

And Otto punches him right in the face.

This got a huge laugh from everyone there. In fact, people laughed at almost every joke. None of the laughter was fake, including mine. Like Gina's comedy set, Otto's web series was the real thing.

When it was all over, I told Otto how much I liked it, that I thought it was really, really great. I sounded sincere, because I *was* sincere.

"But what are you going to do for season two?" I said. "Is 'Otto' in the show going to do a web series about an actor with facial scars?"

Otto laughed. "That's a really good question. I haven't really thought that far ahead. I guess I'll wait and see what people think of the first season."

I leaned in close and lowered my voice a little. "Can I ask you something?"

"Sure. Anything."

"Is 'Otto' gay? The character, I mean. You didn't go into his romantic life at all."

Otto inhaled slowly. "Yeah, I thought about that."

"I'm not judging. I'm just curious."

"I guess I decided that sorta blurred the focus. Which makes me a big freakin' hypocrite, doesn't it? I told those producers how great it would be to have a character who just happens to have scars on his face—that the story wasn't *about* that. And I could do the same thing here, making 'Otto' gay. But it seemed like it confused things, like it would be distracting, exactly what those producers said. It's crazy, isn't it?"

"It's not that crazy," I said.

"But it's not like I gave him a female love interest, you know?" he said. "If I do make a second season, I'm totally going to give 'Otto' a hot boyfriend. You wanna audition?"

For the second time that afternoon, I blushed.

The following week, I was alone in the apartment working on my revisions to *A Cup of Joe*. I was desperately trying to find more obstacles for Joe and Milo's relationship, but everything I'd thought of so far felt trite or overdone.

There was knock on the door. It was the *second* knock we'd had since moving into that apartment.

I knew even before I answered it that it was Daniel again.

"What," I said, not really a question. After the last time he'd been here, he really thought I was going to let him inside again?

He held up his backpack as if that explained everything, then pushed his way past me. I could have stopped him, but it would have meant blocking him with my body, and he was a sexy teenage porcupine: the last thing I wanted to do was touch him.

"Really?" I said.

He ignored me. "Where's your bro?"

"Kevin? He's got an interview. But he should be back any minute."

Daniel flopped down onto the couch again, his legs spread so far apart I thought he was going to rip the crotch of his pants. Those stupid pockets were pulled up again.

"So is he, like, the guy?"

Was Daniel really asking what I thought he was asking?

"Uh, we're both guys," I said.

"Yeah, but you know what I mean."

"I'm not talking about this with you. You're seventeen years old."

"Eighteen."

"What?"

"I turn eighteen. This Sunday."

"Um, that's not really the point. What you're asking is none of your business." And on a related note, why the hell was he assuming *Kevin* was the top in our relationship? (He was wrong, by the way. Well, it sort of depended on what week you asked: it kind of went in waves. But he was *mostly* wrong. Still, I wasn't about to tell Daniel any of this.) "Daniel, what the hell do you want?"

He pulled a textbook from his backpack—*Modern World Studies*, it said—and tossed it onto the couch next to him.

"Yeah," I said. "So?"

"So you said you'd help with my homework. I gotta do the questions at the end of chapter six." He reached for one of the remotes on the table and turned on our television.

I'm not an idiot: I knew he was setting me up. I'd do what he asked, try to help him with his homework, and he'd somehow make fun of me, make me look like a fool. He was six years younger than I was, but he reminded me of the bullies back in my high school. Everyone says that you just need to stand up to bullies and they'll back down, but it's not true. They always win in the end, because winning is more important to them than your looking like an idiot for a few minutes is to you. Being a bully is all they've got, almost by definition. On the other hand, Daniel was smaller than my high school bullies—so small I could probably pick him up like a sack of potatoes and toss him out of the apartment. Still, that would mean actually touching him, and I already explained how I didn't want to do that.

With a sigh, I picked up the textbook and took a seat across from him. I paged through it. The print was bigger than I expected, and I wondered just how much they dumbed things down at Hollywood High these days.

I looked up at Daniel, who had somehow already found a *Saw* movie rip-off in the middle of a particularly gory dismemberment scene. (A pit-trap with chainsaws rather than spikes? Seriously, who comes up with this stuff? On the other hand, maybe a chainsaw pit-trap was exactly what *A Cup of Joe* needed. That was an obstacle that would definitely keep Joe and Milo apart!)

"Daniel," I said, "if you really want my help, you have to turn the TV off."

"Guess what?" he said, not turning the TV off.

"What?"

"This guy says I can be a model."

"What? What guy?"

"This guy I met."

"Daniel..." I said.

"What?"

"Those guys aren't legit." On the other hand, what the hell did I know? Daniel was a good-looking guy. Maybe he really had been stopped by some kind of modeling agent.

On TV, the victim screamed. Daniel watched the limbs fly off in silence.

"Come on," I said. "Turn the TV off."

Incredibly, he turned the TV off, and then came and stood next to my chair, so close I could feel the heat of his body. His crotch, of course, was right at my head level.

*Is this the plan?* I thought. *Flaunt himself at me again?*

"Let's work at the table," I said, standing.

I started for the kitchen, but Daniel went in the other direction—toward Kevin's and my bedroom. I wasn't exactly sure what embarrassing things he might find in there. Our underwear on the bed? Lube on the nightstand? I just knew I didn't want him in there.

"Daniel!" I said, but he completely ignored me and disappeared inside.

I hurried across the apartment.

"*Daniel!*"

As I reached the doorway, he stepped back into the frame, facing me.

We collided. The last thing I'd expected was for

him to listen to me again and do what I'd said, so I stepped right into him like I was walking into a hug. This wasn't just any hug either. It was a full-on, torso-to-torso embrace, almost like he was wrapped around me.

It wasn't erotic exactly.

Okay, I'm lying—it was exactly erotic. Beneath his grimy, rumpled clothing, I could feel him, smaller than me, but just as lean and hard as he'd looked in the pool. And yes, I also felt his crotch, pressing against my thigh. The most surprising thing may have been how he smelled. It was like I'd knocked the pheromones right out of him. Kevin smelled like a man, and Daniel did too, but somehow even fresher. This sounds pervier than I intend, but it was like he'd been plucked off the tree at the exact moment of ripeness.

That, of course, was also the moment when Kevin arrived home.

"I leave for two hours," he said, standing by the door, "and this is what I come home to?"

"Kevin!" I said, trying to untangle myself from Daniel's body—easier said than done. Finally, I pulled away. Somehow my clothes looked rumpled now, like Daniel's always did. I immediately tucked and straightened, even though that probably made me look *more* guilty.

"Daniel went into our bedroom!" I said to Kevin. "He didn't listen when I told him to stop!"

Kevin just smirked.

Daniel was absolutely busting up—"Pendejo!" he said—and I realized I'd been played again. Now he even had Kevin laughing at me.

"Daniel wanted help on some homework," I said.

"*But he was just leaving.*" My face was the death ray in some sci-fi epic.

"Yeah, yeah, I'm going," he said, snatching up his textbook and backpack, then slithering for the door. He'd come, he'd seen, he'd conquered, and now he was leaving.

Kevin stepped to one side to let him go. But when Daniel reached the doorway, he turned back to me and grabbed his crotch through his cotton pants. "That was hot," he said. "But next time, I'm gonna let you do me." Then he was gone.

The second the door was closed, I said, "Nothing happened! I was trying to get him out of our—"

Kevin burst out laughing, but it felt different now that Daniel was gone. Now it felt more like he was laughing at the ridiculousness of the situation.

I smiled.

"You really trust me that much?" I said, touched.

"*Trust* you?" Kevin said. "With Daniel? Oh, hell, no! But I opened the door a few seconds before you think I did. I saw the whole thing."

Later that night, Kevin and I were lying in bed, cuddling. My head was on his chest, and I could smell his athlete's foot cream, which he'd just put on.

"Daniel is such a twit," I said.

"You think he's sexy," Kevin said.

I jerked my head up and glared at him. "I do not!"

"Sure, you do. It's all good. Even if he's only seventeen years old, you pervert."

I didn't say anything for a second. Kevin noticed.

"What?" he said.

"He turns eighteen," I said quietly. "On Sunday."

Kevin laughed.

"Stop that!" I said. "He's a twit."

"Sure, he is. But you still think he's sexy, and now he's basically legal, so just admit it."

"Why don't *you* admit it? You're the one who keeps bringing it up."

"I'm not the one who was pressed up against him in our bedroom today."

I reached down and slipped my hand up through the leg of his running shorts. Kevin wasn't wearing underwear and he was completely hard, straining against the nylon.

I looked back at him accusingly.

"I deny everything," he said.

"Uh huh," I said, gently stroking him. "Maybe you should have a talk with your dick."

"Maybe *you* should have a talk with my dick."

I smiled and leaned in to kiss him. He kissed me back, more forcefully than I expected, hungrily.

*He's still thinking about Daniel*, I thought. But that was okay. I confess I was thinking about Daniel too—the smell of him, the feel of him against my body.

I worked my way down Kevin's torso, sliding his shorts down so I could have that aforementioned conversation with his dick. At the same time, the rest of Kevin's clothes were coming off, and mine were too, even though my mouth barely left his dick.

In a minute, we were both naked, and I climbed on top of him, kissing again, thrusting together. We were touching each other, kissing and licking, but we were thinking about Daniel, even as we both knew the other was thinking about him too.

I couldn't help but wonder: did all gay couples do this? I bet a lot of them did. Unlike straight couples, gay couples can find the exact same person hot. It was totally erotic, knowing that Kevin was turned on by the same thing I was, that we were sharing the same object of desire. In a weird way, both of us thinking about Daniel even made for a strange moment of connection.

The truth is, sex makes no sense whatsoever. But I guess that's a big part of what's so great about it.

Afterward, Kevin fell asleep, but once again I didn't. I just lay in the dark, listening to the traffic and the sounds of the city.

*Whatever you do, don't—*

That's what the ghost said to me before, the last time I'd stayed awake after Kevin and I had sex. Except it wasn't really a ghost. It had probably been the neighbor's radio, a trick of the acoustics.

Still, unlike before, I now knew that someone really had killed himself in our apartment, that screenwriter named Cole Gordon. Or *did* I know that? All I really knew is that there'd once been a screenwriter who'd lived in our building, and he'd died in some kind of accident. I didn't know it was suicide or even that it was our apartment.

I slipped out of bed, pulled on my underwear and a t-shirt, and walked out to the front room. I didn't turn on the lights, or the TV, or even pick up my iPad. I listened, but I didn't hear anything. What was I expecting to hear? The voice of the ghost again? That was stupid.

I looked around the darkened room. If Cole Gordon really had lived here, and he really had committed suicide, I wondered how he'd done it. I'd thought before that maybe he put his head in the oven and turned on the gas, but somehow that didn't feel right.

I looked up at the ceiling, but there wasn't anything to hang a rope on. The only fixture was over the table in the kitchen, and the ceiling wasn't tall enough in there to hang yourself. Could he have put a plastic bag over his head and suffocated himself? Did they even *have* plastic bags in the 1950s? I didn't know. Maybe he took an overdose of sleeping pills—that method of suicide seemed like an old standby.

This line of thinking was morbid. Whatever happened, I had no way of knowing.

The real question was *why* had he done it?

*Gordon, 34, was an unproduced screenwriter.*

That's all the article said. Was I jumping to conclusions to assume that he'd killed himself *because* he was an unproduced screenwriter? That's what the legend said—what Gina had told us that day we first met her—but I wasn't sure if I should put any stock in that at all. Weren't legends like that game you play at birthday parties, where you go around the room whispering in each other's ears, and by the end of the game, the person says something completely different from what the first person whispered?

Still, I thought, let's assume that really was the ghost of Cole Gordon I heard: a *big* assumption, but whatever. Presumably, it was hard for ghosts to speak to the living. If it wasn't, they'd talk to us a lot more often, and more importantly, someone would have *proved* that they talk to us. Maybe this particular ghost had gotten through to me anyway, at least for a few seconds. What was so important that he had to try and reach me? And what was the rest of the sentence?

It had sounded like a warning.

Cole Gordon was a screenwriter, and I was a screenwriter, so it seemed reasonable to assume it had something to do with that. Did it have to do with my movie deal with Mr. Brander? Was I making a mistake somehow?

"Tell me," I said to the darkness. "What's the thing that's so important I not do?"

The second I said the words out loud, I felt stupid again. It was definitely time to go back to bed. I'm not the smartest guy in the world, but even I knew it was time to turn in when you were standing in a darkened room, listening for answers that will never come.

I closed the bedroom door behind me.

Of course, once I was in bed, I immediately had another thought: *Maybe I closed that door for a reason.* Maybe I didn't *want* to talk to the ghost because somehow I knew he was trying to tell me something I really didn't want to hear.

# CHAPTER ELEVEN

The following Saturday night, Kevin and I were invited over to Mr. Brander's house for a dinner party. As we drove over there, I was back to being nervous.

Weirdly, I think I was mostly nervous because Kevin was with me. I never had told him what happened that day at the theater. But now I was worried about how Mr. Brander would act in front of him. Would it be like the first two times I'd met him? Or would it be like the reading when he'd seemed so befuddled, at least at first? Kevin didn't understand how movies were made—the Bullshit Factor, the Screenwriter Loophole. He didn't know how crazy everyone could be, that it was sometimes a messy process.

"Just so you know," I said as we drove. "Mr. Brander is kind of strange."

"So you've said. What do you mean?"

What *did* I mean?

"Well, he's kind of full of himself," I said. "He might be the most confident person I've ever met."

"Yeah?"

"Oh, yeah. You could bounce a quarter off his ego."

This was true, but it wasn't what I'd been trying to tell Kevin.

We drove in silence a bit, and I guess Kevin noticed something was wrong, because he said, "You okay?"

I nodded.

"You'll be fine," he said. "Remember before the first meeting? You were nervous then too, but you ended up being great."

I nodded again, still not telling him what I was really thinking.

Lewis greeted us at the front door. I was glad Kevin and I had decided to wear jackets, because he was dressed up too.

"Kevin, this is Lewis," I said, and the two of them shook hands.

"Nice to meet you," Kevin said.

"So do you actually live here?" I said to Lewis, before I realized it wasn't any of my damn business.

But he didn't seem to take offense. "I do," he said.

He led us into the front room where Mr. Brander was waiting for us in his wheelchair. There were hors d'oeuvres on the coffee table: some kind of puff pastry, and crackers and dip. The music on the player was classical, relatively upbeat, but I don't know anything about classical music, so let's just say it was Mozart.

"Russel, my boy!" he said. He turned to take Kevin in. "And you must be Kevin."

"It's great to meet you," Kevin said, shaking Mr. Brander's hand. "I've heard a lot about you."

"I don't know anything about you, but I feel like I do"—he smiled at me—"from reading Russel's screenplay."

"Yeah, that's the problem with living with a writer," Kevin said. "You never know when something you do or say will end up in one of their scripts."

"Well, if you're at all like Milo, I like you already."

As they talked, I reached for a puffed pastry, not because I wanted an hors d'oeuvre, but so I could step closer to Mr. Brander to see if he still smelled like, well, you know. He didn't, which was a relief, though he did smell a bit menthol-y. I'd also never told Kevin about how Mr. Brander had smelled before.

"Lewis?" the old man said. "Shall we have the drinks now?"

"Sure thing," Lewis said,

After he left, Mr. Brander said, "Please! Sit."

Kevin and I sat.

"So Kevin, my boy," Mr. Brander said. "Do you like movies?"

"Oh, sure," Kevin said. "But not as much as Russel does. I just sort of watch them, you know? He drinks them down like cups of coffee."

"Well put!" Mr. Brander said. He sized Kevin up. "Are you a Sean Connery fan?"

"Sure," Kevin said.

"I worked with the man. Right in the middle of the Bond years too. I've always said that smart actors can play dumb, but a truly dumb actor can't play smart. Well, Sean Connery was the one exception."

"Oh, no," Kevin said. "Really?"

Mr. Brander shook his head sadly. "But he looks *fantastic* in a tux."

I knew what Mr. Brander was doing: he was trying to impress Kevin with stories from his past, name-dropping the celebrity he thought would most impress the person he was talking to. (What did it mean that Kevin got Sean Connery while I'd gotten Bette Davis?!)

But the fact is, Kevin *did* look impressed. Mr. Brander's plan worked. So I was finally starting to relax, thinking that maybe this evening would go okay after all.

"What was the movie you did together?" Kevin asked Mr. Brander, still talking Sean Connery.

I stood up. "Excuse me a sec," I said as if I needed to use the bathroom. But instead, I looked around the house for Lewis.

I found him in the kitchen wrestling with a bottle of champagne. He'd wrapped a towel around the cork and was trying to ease it out.

"Sorry about before," I said to him.

"For what?" he said, even as he kept working on the cork.

"For asking if you live here. That's none of my business."

He smiled. "It's fine. I've worked for Mr. Brander for almost two years now."

The cork slid out with almost no pop and none of the foam that oozes out whenever I open a bottle of champagne. Lewis had a light touch. Food containers littered the countertops, along with plates in a stack: Mr. Brander had had tonight's dinner catered, and presumably Lewis would be the one to assemble it. It smelled fantastic.

Lewis started pouring the champagne into flutes—crystal ones, it looked like, old and expensive.

"Can I help you with anything?" I said.

"Nope," he said. "I've got it."

"Okay..." I turned back toward the front room.

"Russel?" Lewis said.

"Yeah?" I said, turning back toward him.

He stared at me, but didn't say anything.

*He wants to tell me something,* I thought. *That he doesn't just work for Mr. Brander, but that the two of them are some kind of couple. But he thinks I'll judge him.*

"What is it?" I said.

He looked away. Then he said, "There's a mountain lion living in Griffith Park."

"Huh?" Griffith Park is this massive greenbelt right in the middle of the city—part of the Hollywood Hills, and also where the big "Hollywood" sign is located. But I didn't understand what it had to do with anything.

"I guess it's been living there for years," Lewis went on. "They say it had to cross sixteen lanes of freeway." As he talked, he finished filling the glasses. He acted like he was totally transfixed on that champagne, getting each glass filled just right. He seemed nervous. The thing about the mountain lion? That wasn't what he'd been trying to tell me. How could I tell him that I didn't judge other people's living arrangements?

"Yeah, I heard that," I said, meaning the stuff about the lion. "Seriously, do you need me to help carry the drinks?"

"No, it's fine," he said, turning his back on me, looking for something in one of the cupboards, dismissing me.

*Oh, well,* I thought. Whatever the deal was between the two of them, it wasn't any of my business.

Back in the front room, Kevin and Mr. Brander were laughing. They really had hit it off! The music on the player had segued into something darker, smokier, but just as old-fashioned. A tango?

I joined them and Mr. Brander nodded to the hors d'oeuvres. "Try the eggplant caviar," he said. "Lewis made it."

"*Eggplant* caviar?" I said.

He chuckled. "Well, I'm not rich enough for the real stuff anymore. But maybe I will be again, once we make this movie."

I tried it on a cracker. I have no idea if it was as good as real caviar, because I've never had it, but this stuff wasn't bad. It had garlic and lemon.

"When does everyone else get here?" I said.

"Everyone else?" Mr. Brander said.

"The other people. For dinner?"

"There are no other people. It's just us tonight."

"Oh." This confused me. On the phone, Lewis had said it was a dinner party, so I'd assumed others would be there—the whole production team.

Kevin looked at me. Had I told him that I'd thought everyone else was coming too? I couldn't remember, but I smiled like it wasn't any big deal.

Right then, Lewis arrived with the champagne flutes on a tray, which he distributed to Mr. Brander,

Kevin, and me. There was a glass for him too, and I was glad, because I would've felt awkward with the three of us drinking and Lewis watching us.

"To *A Cup of Joe*!" Mr. Brander said, raising a glass.

"*A Cup of Joe*!" Kevin said, drinking.

Champagne? A catered dinner? Even if it was eggplant caviar and not the real thing, Mr. Brander had gone to a lot of trouble for this night, and it was all for me. People were literally toasting my success. Moments like this didn't come very often in life, and I knew I should be flattered.

So why was I still so nervous?

Dinner was better than it deserved to be, given that Lewis had reheated it in the kitchen. It was chicken Marsala with wild mushrooms, roasted potatoes, and a vegetable medley. Mr. Brander may not have been rich now, but he must have been at one point: the china was definitely fine and had what I was pretty sure was real gold trim.

As we all ate, the wine flowed freely, the candlesticks flickered, and Mr. Brander did what he did best: talked.

"There are actually two Hollywoods," he told us. "There's the one that Middle America knows about: the movie stars, and the glamour, and the gossip. That's all most people care about, which is fine. And by all means: actors are pretty to look at, fun to watch. That's an important part of the business model, the public face. But actors have almost nothing to do with the actual making of movies. Of all the principals, the actors spend the least amount of time on a film. They leave the real work, the *hard* work, to the second Hollywood: the producers, the directors, and"—here he nodded to me—"the writers. We find the ideas, we create them right out of thin air. And we work on them from the very beginning, back when no one else gives a damn. But we have faith in each other, and we have trust. And so, like pioneers across the frontier, we follow the project through, across rivers and over mountains, to the end of the trail, hoping against hope that there will be someone waiting for us there, a civilization at the end of the wildness that will understand us—that will welcome our vision."

I looked at Kevin and tried to communicate with my eyes: *Remember what I said about Mr. Brander being full of himself?* But I couldn't tell what he was thinking.

It was also interesting to hear what Mr. Brander thought of actors, that they were basically a necessary evil. Well, why not? Otto had told me what actors think of writers: that we're mostly hideous beasts with zero social skills.

"It's actually really frustrating for journalists," Kevin said to Mr. Brander.

"That's right, you interview celebrities," Mr. Brander said. "And how does that go?"

"Well, it's true what you're saying," he said. "It's the writer, the director, and the producer who have the interesting things to say about the movie. Sometimes the actor doesn't know anything at all. But no one wants to read an interview with the *producer* or the *writer* of a movie. They want to know what the movie star has to say. So you end up with all this great material you can barely use. And then you go through and try to find the one interesting thing the movie star said. Because that's the other thing no one wants to read, and no editor wants to see either: an article about how everyone's favorite movie star is actually a complete idiot."

"Like Sean Connery?" Mr. Brander said.

Kevin smirked. "You said it, not me."

Mr. Brander laughed. "You can take my word for it!" He pointed a fork at Kevin. "But you're so right, my boy. Absolutely right!"

I smiled too, but to myself. Kevin wasn't lying exactly—he'd said stuff like that to me before—but mostly he knew how to work an audience.

*He's enjoying this!* I thought. *The evening is going great.*

When we were done with dinner, after Lewis had cleared the dishes and we were having dessert and coffee, Mr. Brander nodded to Lewis, and he brought me a package.

"What's this?" I said.

"Just a little something I wanted you to have," Mr. Brander said.

I unwrapped it. It was a paperback copy of *The Glass Menagerie*, really old. I opened the cover. It was signed by Tennessee Williams.

"Mr. Brander!" I said. "You can't give me this!"

"Of course I can. Tennessee gave it to me, and I'm giving it to you."

"But—"

"Russel, please. It would make me very happy for you to have it."

"Well, thank you," I said, genuinely touched. "I mean it. Thanks a lot."

"No, thank *you*. I meant what I said before: good writers don't get nearly the attention they deserve."

This wasn't exactly what he'd said before, but it

was close enough. I glanced at Kevin, who smiled at me. Suddenly I felt stupid for feeling so uneasy about the dinner, and Kevin, and the whole movie project.

"But my real gift to you," Mr. Brander said to me, "is the news I have to share. I hope you'll forgive me for waiting this long to tell you."

"Really?" I made a mock-impatient face. "Yes, yes, I forgive you, now what the hell *is* it!?"

Mr. Brander laughed. "Well, what do you think of Shirley MacLaine as the grandmother?"

At that exact moment, I couldn't think of any specific Shirley MacLaine movies. (Now I can: *The Apartment. Terms of Endearment.* And *Steel Magnolias.*) But even then, I knew she had once been a really big movie star.

"Why?" I said, a little confused.

Mr. Brander beamed. "Because I sent her the script, and she loved it, and she wants to do it!"

"She wants to do *A Cup of Joe*?"

"She wants to do *A Cup of Joe*!"

I didn't know what to say. A famous movie star was going to perform words I'd written? Better still, having Shirley MacLaine on board had to mean that the movie was far more likely to get made—that she would legitimize the project and attract investors and other stars.

"I don't know what to say," I said. "I'm stunned. That's fantastic!"

"It's not official yet," Mr. Brander said. "But she loved the script. We still need to hammer out the details. Just think of it: Sally Field in our little movie!"

Kevin and I didn't say anything. A thread of wax from one of the candles slid down onto the tablecloth. The candles had burned more than half-way. The one that had dripped was also smoking.

In the awkward silence that followed, Lewis stood up and started clearing the dessert dishes.

"Sally Field?" Kevin said at last.

"Yes," Mr. Brander said smugly. "She's won two Oscars, you know."

"Before you said Shirley MacLaine."

Mr. Brander stared at him for a second. "What?"

"You said it was Shirley MacLaine as the grand-mother, then you said it was Sally Field."

Mr. Brander's forehead wrinkled. "No. Did I? I'm sorry. It's Sally Field. I worked with her before, you know. What was the movie? Lewis? What was the movie I did with Sally Field?"

But Lewis was gone. He'd carried that first load of dishes into the kitchen.

"Well," I said, suddenly standing. "This has been great—*really* great—but Kevin and I should probably get moving."

"Oh?" Mr. Brander said, palpably disappointed. "Very well. But we'll be doing this again very soon, of course."

Kevin followed my lead and stood up too.

"Russel, my boy," Mr. Brander said. He pointed to the table. "Don't forget your book."

"Oh, right," I said, taking the book and quickly turning for the exit.


Once in the car, we drove in silence for at least five minutes. I knew what Kevin was thinking—about Mr.

Brander's confusing Sally Field with Shirley MacLaine. I also knew he was going to make a big deal about it, and it really hadn't been anything at all.

So I said, "What do you want to do tomorrow? We haven't been up the coast yet."

"Sure."

Kevin drove in silence a few seconds longer.

"Did you think—?" he started to say.

"It was nothing," I said. "He just got confused."

"What did you think I was going to say?"

"Something about how he confused Shirley Mac-Laine with Sally Field. But it was a simple mistake. He talked about Sally Field before. That's who it was all along."

"When?"

"What?"

"When before?"

"The first meeting," I said. "Or maybe the second one, I don't remember. But I know he told me he was really good friends with her. He just gets a little confused sometimes."

"Confused how?"

"Well, I mean, he's eighty-thousand years old. But it's fine. It's all good, like you always say."

Kevin didn't respond, and we drove on.

I faked a laugh. "That's quite a house, isn't it? Going over to Mr. Brander's feels a little like being invited to the estate of a billionaire, like he's offering us a million dollars to spend the night in a haunted mansion."

Unlike the producers that one time, Kevin didn't laugh. He just kept staring out at the road in front of us.

"And what's the deal with Lewis?" I said, fake-laughing again. "I mean, are the two of them a couple or what?"

Kevin smiled, but only a little.

We stopped at a traffic light. Kevin sat stiffly at the wheel.

"What?" I said, a little exasperated.

Kevin looked over at me, confused.

"Tell me what you're thinking," I said.

"I'm not thinking anything."

"You're obviously thinking *something*."

He thought for a second. Then he said, "How confused?"

"Who?" I said. "Mr. Brander? It's nothing. He sometimes has a problem with names. It's hardly noticeable."

"Is that why no one else showed up tonight? Because Mr. Brander screwed something up?"

"What? No! That was *my* fault. I got that wrong."

"It feels like there's something off."

I tried to laugh, but it came out like more of a cough. "There's nothing off."

"Has he paid you yet?"

"What?"

"The option money," Kevin said. "Have you got the check yet?"

"I don't know, that would go to Fiona. But it doesn't matter. Otto says that in Hollywood, everything always takes three times longer than you think it will."

"But—"

Something snapped in me. "*Stop it!* Why do you have to be so damn negative all the time?"

"I'm not—"

"That was really special tonight, Mr. Brander

toasting me and my movie, and later giving me that book. Can't you just let me appreciate it for five minutes? Do you really have to crap all over it right now?"

The light changed to green, and Kevin started forward again.

"I'm sorry," Kevin said.

"No, I'm sorry," I said. "I overreacted."

"No, but you're right. This was your evening. I was being stupid."

"It's okay."

It's not like we rode the rest of the way home in silence. We went on talking, and I did my best to act like I'd forgiven Kevin. But the fact is, when someone says the one thing you really don't want to hear, it's hard to forgive them, at least right away.

## CHAPTER TWELVE

The next morning, Sunday, Kevin was waiting for me when I woke me up.

"Take a shower and get dressed," he said.

"Huh?" I said, groggy.

"Come on. There's something I wanna show you."

So I took a shower, got dressed, had a quick breakfast, and then got into the car with Kevin, who drove us through the city out to the coast.

We chatted, and everything was casual, but the truth is, I was still a little miffed about the night before, about what Kevin had said about Mr. Brander. But I was trying not to be.

Kevin drove us up the Pacific Coast Highway to Malibu. It was Sunday, and traffic was slightly less horrible than usual. We passed Cher's villa, which is partially visible from the street, but I didn't say anything about it to Kevin.

Finally, we pulled into a park right along the water called Westward Beach (near Zuma Beach). Kevin climbed out of the car, but I stared out at the water for a second. The beach was long and sandy, with occasional lifeguard stations. It was a Sunday afternoon in early November, and the weather was good but not great, so it was crowded but not insane.

"Come on," Kevin said.

"Where are we going?" I said. I admit I was curious.

"You'll see."

So he led me down to the beach, then south along the water.

Eventually we reached a rocky promontory jutting out into the ocean, steep and sharp, like the fin of a shark. There was a jumble of boulders at the base, and the water washed against them.

"We need to climb around the point," Kevin said.

"Why?" I said.

"Trust me," he said. "Okay?"

I confess now I was incredibly curious. Where was Kevin taking me? He'd never done anything like this before.

We climbed over the boulders and onto another beach beyond. It wasn't quite a cove—the curve was more gentle than that, but the cliff face continued down along the sand. The beach itself was cut off from roads and houses by that cliff, making it seem sheltered and protected, isolated even. As far as I could tell, short of climbing down the cliffs or coming in by boat, there was no way into this little half-cove other than the way we'd just come.

A couple hundred yards down the beach, Kevin stopped.

"Do you know where we are?" he asked me.

I turned all the way around, but I didn't have a clue. "A beach in Malibu?"

"Technically, Point Dume. But take another look." He pointed to the cliff face again. "There." Then he pointed down the beach in front of us. "And over there."

I looked where he was pointing, but nothing seemed familiar.

I shook my head at him.

Suddenly Kevin collapsed into sand at the edge of the surf, as if in despair. "Oh, my God. I'm back. I'm home. All the time, it was Earth. We finally *really* did it."

At first I didn't understand what was happening, what Kevin was doing. Then I realized: he was giving me his best Charlton Heston overacting. It was the final line from the original *Planet of the Apes* (a movie I loved, something Kevin knew).

"*You maniacs!*" Kevin wailed, still quoting the movie. "You blew it up! Ah, damn you! God *damn* you all to *hell*!"

I looked back at those cliffs, at the beach in front of me, finally clueing in. "This is where they filmed that final scene. But it's different..."

Kevin stood up again, brushed himself off. "Well, obviously there's no Statue of Liberty. And it's been, like, fifty years since they shot the movie."

Was it really possible? Kevin knew something about movies I didn't? Something about Los Angeles movie locations?

He pointed to the cliff face. "That's also the site of Tony Stark's mansion in *Iron Man*."

I gave Kevin my first official smile since the day before. "You looked all this up? For me?"

"I wanted to say I'm sorry about last night. For what I said about Mr. Brander. I was being a dud."

Now I felt stupid. I'd overreacted. Kevin hadn't said anything wrong. He was just concerned about me. And he was right: Mr. Brander, the whole situation with him, some things *were* weird.

"You don't have anything to apologize for," I said. "I'm the one who should be apologizing."

"Still."

I thought for a second. "One thing. If you really thought you had something to apologize for, how come you didn't actually get in the surf like Charlton Heston does in the movie?"

"Well, I didn't wanna get wet," Kevin said. "I mean, come on, I don't love you *that* much."

I laughed out loud. We were back to teasing each other, and things were good again. It really was fun—not only seeing this beach, being in the exact spot where they filmed the best movie ending of all time, but also being here with Kevin, having him do this for me, because he knew how much I'd like it.

"Thanks," I said, pulling him close, kissing him.

On our walk back to the car, I saw two other people quote Charlton Heston's speech from the end of *Planet of the Apes* (one guy actually *in* the surf).

Once we got to the car, I said, "We're totally good, and you didn't do anything you needed to apologize for anyway. But..."

Kevin smiled. "What?"

"Well, if you want to build up even more bonus points to spend on future fights, we could stop at Malibu State Park on the way home."

"We could, could we?" he said, laughing. "Why?"

"Because that's where they filmed the rest of the first *Planet of the Apes* movies. And also a whole bunch of other stuff, like *Logan's Run* and all the Tarzan movies." I'd looked all this up on my phone just then.

"Is there anything to see?" he asked.

"The actual movie sets are all long gone—they blew them up, God damn them all to hell!—but you can make out the mountain that stands in the background of Ape Village."

Kevin laughed. "So that'll get me in good, huh?"

"Oh, *yeah*," I said. "Completely!"

"Well," he said, like he was the dad and I was the ten-year-old boy, "then I guess we'll just have to stop."

On Monday, Tuesday, and Wednesday of the following week, Otto was filming all five episodes of his web series, and I volunteered to help. We used Otto's actual bedroom and bathroom at the Hive for "Otto's" bedroom and bathroom. Exterior locations were all done in the streets and a park near the house, and Otto called in some favors and got permission to film at a nearby grocery store, a couple of office buildings, and a coffee shop.

Otto and his housemates and friends played all the roles, and another couple of his friends acted as the director and script supervisor. I wasn't offended that Otto hadn't asked me to play any of the parts (except a non-speaking background extra now and then), because I'm a terrible actor. I also didn't know goat shit about filmmaking, so I ended up as a "production assistant," which is basically someone who does all the grunt work that everyone else is too busy or important to do: holding lights, carrying equipment, and cleaning up the two-liter bottle of Pepsi when some idiot leaves it on the floor, open, and then some other idiot comes along and accidentally kicks it into the office hallway.

It was more work than I expected, like helping someone pack and move three days in a row. But Otto was my friend, and I was (mostly) happy to help.

Eventually, it was Wednesday night. Everyone else was gone, back to their own houses, their own rooms, but I'd stayed behind to help Otto clean up the last of the mess (the first time those rooms at the Hive had *ever* been cleaned, I think).

"I think that went really well," he said, meaning the whole shoot.

"Oh, yeah," I said. "The stuff I saw? It looked really, really good. It was fun watching you."

"What's strange is that I'm playing myself, but I still think of him as an actual character. Not me, you know?"

I laughed. "I guess it sort of *is* a character. It isn't really you." I looked around his bedroom, where we happened to be right then: we were cleaned up at last. "Well, I should go. The good news is that by working so long, I think I missed the traffic."

He smiled. "Thanks for your help. Really. All my other friends? They'll do anything to get in front of a camera, any camera, so it's not like they're doing me that big a favor. But you—you're not getting anything out of this. You're just here to help. And, I mean, I'm sorry about the Pepsi."

"It was fun," I said. "I learned a lot."

I stepped closer and hugged him. That close, I could smell him. I'd hugged him since I moved to Los Angeles, but it had always been on the street or in spicy ethnic restaurants. I'd never been able to smell him, not the way I could now. He was a complicated mixture of smells, but ultimately something clean and fun, like Play-Dough.

I pulled back, but not that far. My face was only inches from his face. I could still smell him. Suddenly I was aware that the door to his bedroom was closed.

Otto and I stared at each other.

I looked at his face. His scar had long since become invisible to me again, and I wasn't seeing it now either. I was just seeing "Otto"—the tousle of his hair, the sly cut of his lips, those great, brown-burgundy eyes. I liked Otto as a teenager, maybe even truly loved him, but as great as he'd been then, he was so much more than that now: a supportive friend, a dedicated actor, a surprisingly good writer, someone who'd been able to pull this whole web series together in just a matter of weeks. Otto was someone who knew who he was, what he wanted, and that was always attractive.

As we looked at each other, I saw something else too. Lately, I'd been imagining all kinds of things: seeing the past lives of the people who had lived in my apartment, hearing the ghost of Cole Gordon. Now I got a glimpse into another dimension—a different timeline, I guess.

*Otto and I are a couple. We met at summer camp when we were both sixteen years old, and we never broke up. We have somehow made it work, seeing each other on weekends and spending whole weeks together in the summers. I'd always loved movies, but for once I am spending time with someone who loves them the same way I do, with a passion bordering on obsessive. Just the mere act of being with someone so like me in this respect is opening boxes inside myself—boxes within boxes within boxes.*

I wasn't just seeing *into* this other timeline. It was like the two timelines were somehow converging, joining together like the two sides of a long ribbon, once pulled apart, but now meeting face to face. I was somehow living in both timelines at once.

*Otto and I ended up going to college together—I'd moved down to Los Angeles at the end of my sophomore year to be with him, to go to UCLA. We'd both discovered our vocations in the arts—his desire to be an actor, mine to be a screenwriter—and we lived in this crazy town together all through school and after, chasing our dreams, doing exactly what we were meant to do.*

Our lips were so close together, just inches apart. But neither of us moved. I could feel the warm gusts of air from his nose on my cheek, smell his sweet breath.

*Today had occurred almost exactly as I remembered it. Otto had filmed the third day of his web series, and I'd helped him, and now we were finishing cleaning up together afterward. But I'm not about to leave, to go home to Kevin, because Kevin doesn't exist in this timeline, at least not in Los Angeles. He is back in Seattle, still living with his ex-boyfriend Colin. In this timeline, it is Otto I love, Otto I have always loved. I can see it in Otto's eyes too: that I am the one he shares his passion with.*

I could see it in Otto's eyes for real. I wasn't the only one seeing into this other timeline, experiencing these feelings.

*In this new timeline, Otto and I have kissed recently, many times. And now, at the end of a hard day's work, we are about to kiss again. We are both tired, exhausted actually, but the kiss will energize us, especially as it grows more passionate. Sex with Otto, I know, is like gunpowder, like a powder keg: once it starts burning, it takes on a life of its own, burning brighter, hotter, until it explodes. The Hive is our house, the place where we live together, and this is our bedroom, our bed. Midway into the kiss, Otto will take my hand, pull me toward the bed, and we will undress—not a sly seduction, or the eager fumblings of a couple that hasn't had sex together since high school. Instead, it will be the casual shucking of clothes that comes after years together, a familiarity that is perhaps too easy, but also so comfortable. Our bodies, so used to each other now, will fall onto the sheets of our futon, and we will make love the way we have so many times before.*

Everything froze. This was the exact moment where the two timelines met. Like the timeline itself, Otto and I were one. Could we go on being one? Could I jump from one timeline to the other? In that instant, I was certain it was possible. So what if the past of our new timeline got jumbled, if it wouldn't be exactly clear when we'd gotten together, where I'd gone to college, where I'd live these past few years. The point is, we could go on living together, sharing our lives, chasing our dreams.

We still didn't move. I realized that neither of us had moved for a long time, ten seconds or more, not even blinking.

*Whatever you do, don't kiss the ex-boyfriend.*

Maybe this was what the ghost of Cole Gordon had been trying to tell me that night in our apartment. Except at that point, he wouldn't have had any way of knowing about Otto. Even so, it was still good advice.

So I blinked. I said to Otto, "Well, I should probably get going."

"Oh, yeah!" he said, pulling back. "Definitely."

Just like that, the timelines were splitting apart again. The moment had broken. The connection we'd shared, our glimpse into that other timeline? It was gone now. What existed in that dimension didn't exist in this one, and now it never would.

But I was glad I'd shared that moment with Otto. He and I had loved each other once, but we were friends now, and that was a very good thing for both of us to know. In a way, it also felt like I'd finally truly moved on from the things Kevin had said after that dinner with Mr. Brander, like he and I were completely good again.

When I got home that night, Kevin was baking cookies, which meant the landlord had finally fixed the oven.

"Oh, my God, that smells so good!" I said. The first batch of cookies was already done, on a plate on the counter. "Snickerdoodles!"

"I looked up a recipe online," he said, smiling.

I had one. It was fantastic, warm and buttery. (He'd overdone the cinnamon and underdone the sugar in the cinnamon-sugar coating, but I wasn't about to point that out.)

"They're great!" I said, loving the fact that he'd baked them for me, and also the fact that he baked cookies at all. We teased each other about which one of us was the butchest, but Kevin had been right when he'd said that the sexiest thing of all was a guy who didn't get hung up about how butch he was.

"How'd it go with the web series? You're finally done now, right?"

"Yeah," I said, and then I went on to tell him about the day's shoot. I didn't mention the moment

I'd had with Otto in his bedroom, mostly because there really wasn't anything to mention. We hadn't kissed. We hadn't really even almost-kissed.

"I think I made a decision," I said.

"Yeah?" Kevin said.

"I'm going to email Fiona Lang."

"To see what she thinks of your screenplays?"

I nodded. "It's crazy. It's been, like, six weeks. And"—here I gave Kevin an apologetic look—"I can also ask her about the check from Mr. Brander."

There was a knock at the door.

Daniel, of course.

"¿Pero qué chingados?" he said. I think he meant the cookies, that he thought they smelled good, but with him, who the hell knows?

"What do you need?" I said, not particularly amused by having this cocky kid intrude on my moment with Kevin.

"Your shower," he said.

"What?" I was confused.

"Our shower don't work." He was carrying a rolled-up beach towel, but I guess I assumed he was on his way to the pool.

I looked at Kevin, in the kitchen doorway again. Before Kevin could even shrug, Daniel was sauntering across the floor toward our bathroom. Part of me wanted to stop him, ask him more questions: "What's wrong with your shower?" And, "Does your sister know you're here?"

I was too late. Before I could speak, he disappeared into the bathroom, and I heard the shower start. (But—and this seemed important somehow—he hadn't closed the door all the way.)

Steam billowed out the crack of that open door.

I stepped closer to Kevin. The door to the bathroom was open, and I didn't want Daniel overhearing us talking. But I didn't know what to say exactly. I mean, maybe Daniel really did need to use our shower.

Kevin's eyes met mine. He was thinking the same thing I was. Given the way Daniel had been acting around us, having him naked in our bathroom was not a good thing. But what could we do? He was already naked, and slick with water by now, probably soaping up his whole body.

*Oy.*

The point is, it's not like we could go in there and pull him out of the shower.

A minute or so later, the water stopped.

The door opened, and Daniel stepped out. He had his towel wrapped around his waist. His skin was still wet, sleek and glistening. More importantly, he was getting water all over our floor.

"Daniel!" I said. "Stop!"

"What?" he said, clueless, or pretending to be.

"You didn't even dry off."

"Oh. Lo siento."

The instant before he did it, I knew what he was going to do—that he was going to pull the towel off from around his waist and start drying off right in front of us.

Yup. He was standing there completely starkers.

He flopped the towel over his head and started drying his hair. It was a total tease, of course. He was giving us the chance to look at him without him knowing, so we could stare outright. Except he *did* know we were looking.

I'd like to say I turned my eyes away, but I didn't.

He dried his hair more vigorously now, and his cock swung from side to side. It was already thicker than it had been a moment before. He was getting a hard-on.

I glanced at Kevin. As our eyes met, we shared a moment, a little like the one I'd shared with Otto back in his bedroom. Maybe it was even another diverging of the timelines, a point where things could go one of two different ways.

I stepped forward toward Daniel.

He spread his legs, bracing them, leaning back against the wall with one hand.

I bent down, my head only inches from his dick, which was already almost fully hard. Once again, I could feel its heat.

*Whatever you do, don't fuck the hot teenage boy next door.*

Maybe *this* was what Cole Gordon had been trying to tell me that night. Even if it wasn't, once again it was really good advice.

I picked up the wet towel and wrapped it around Daniels waist, tucking it tight.

Daniel looked confused, like it hadn't occurred to him that our rejecting him was even a possibility.

Maybe in that other timeline, it hadn't been. Who knows what the three of us might have done there?

But that was that timeline, not this one. In this timeline, it was clear that there was something off about Daniel—that he wanted something from Kevin and me, but for the wrong reasons. He wasn't here because he was attracted to us or wanted to have a casual fling. He was here because he had questions about his sexuality, or because he wanted to piss off his sister. Hell, maybe he just wanted to embarrass me again.

I stepped back from Daniel and stood next to Kevin, the two of us in solidarity.

Daniel looked back and forth between us again, still confused, embarrassed, and also more than a little angry. Then he turned for the bathroom to get dressed again. I could hear him in there, growing angry, so mad that I could hear the *whoosh* of his pants as he pulled them on.

When he stepped out of the bathroom again, I said, "Daniel, stop. Let's talk, okay?"

He didn't talk. He didn't even stop. He burrowed right for the door.

"Daniel!" Kevin said, reaching for him. "Please stop!"

Daniel squirmed away. He tried to slam the door behind him, but it got caught on a piece of carpet just inside the door.

When he was gone, Kevin finally closed the door and faced me.

"That kid has *issues*," Kevin said.

"Serious ones," I said.

"So what do we do? Talk to Zoe?"

"I don't know. Somehow it feels like she's part of the reason he was up here in the first place. We can mention we're concerned, but she'll just ask why. And telling her what happened, that seems like it'd make things even worse. Besides, isn't that, like, outing him?"

"Still. We should do something."

It *did* feel like we should do something.

"But what?" I said. "I mean, apart from being here if he needs to talk."

Kevin kept thinking. I did too.

"I hate to say it," I said, "but if he doesn't want our

help, I don't see what we can do. I mean, you can't really save someone from himself."

Kevin didn't say anything, and my words hung in the air, longer than I wanted, sounding harsher than I intended.

It was stuffy in that apartment, but I shivered.

It wasn't only Daniel I felt bad about. After all, if it was really true that other people couldn't save us from ourselves, that meant we were all pretty much on our own, including me.

# CHAPTER THIRTEEN

Friday morning, Kevin told me he had a press junket at the Beverly Hilton for an upcoming movie.

"Wait," I said. "Is that the hotel Ellen says we should boycott because it's owned by that sultan who wants to stone gay people?"

"No, that's the Beverly Hills Hotel," Kevin said. "The Beverly Hilton is where Whitney Houston drowned in the bathtub."

"Can I come?"

"Because Whitney Houston died there? It's not like there's a shrine."

"Actually, I think people still do leave flowers outside. But that's not why I want to go."

"Then why?"

"Because I've never seen it, and my week's already screwed the pooch because of all that time I spent helping Otto."

"But it'll be boring. You don't have a press pass, so you can't get into any of the events."

"I'll bring the laptop," I said. "I'll wait in the bar."

"For three hours?"

"Sure."

"Okay," Kevin said with a shrug. "It's all good."

A movie junket is when the movie studios invite all the entertainment journalists to a big hotel, and then they also bring in all the movie's stars. If you're important enough—a TV journalist, or someone from one of the big daily newspapers—you might get to spend ten or fifteen minutes alone with the movie star in one of the hotel rooms (accompanied by a publicist, of course). If you're a less important journalist, like a blogger or a writer for a small newspaper, you have to be content with attending the big press conference, where the movie stars take questions from the audience, and maybe you'll also get a few minutes with the movie star at a round-robin table with five or so other writers. (The writer, director, and producer of the movie are all usually at press junkets too, and they always have interesting things to say, but it's like what Kevin said that night at dinner: unless the director is named "Steven Spielberg" or "Quentin Tarantino," no one gives a mouse's fart.)

The point is that all these writers and TV people can go home and boast to their readers or viewers how they got an "exclusive" interview with an actual movie star, making them look much more connected and important than they actually are. When it comes to Hollywood, everyone employs the Bullshit Factor, even the writers who write about us.

When we got to the hotel, Kevin bee-lined off to his press event. I decided to linger in the lobby. I'd been wrong: there were no longer any flowers outside for Whitney Houston. But I figured I might still run into a famous face or two. That happens everywhere in Los Angeles. Our very first week there, Kevin and I had seen Lena Headey—Cersei on *Game of Thrones*—in the produce section at Ralphs. But your odds are better at places like the Beverly Hilton, especially when it's the setting for a press junket for a movie starring Jennifer Lawrence, Bradley Cooper, and Julianne Moore.

I made a quick scan of the lobby. In my mind, people immediately fell into three categories: industry types who just happened to be in the lobby of the hotel for business; publicists and studio people involved with the movie junket; and the journalists who'd come to the junket.

Everyone looked tanned and toned and pretty, except for the writers who mostly looked like pudgy, pathetic dorks. I was starting to get annoyed by how right Otto had been about both the Bullshit Factor *and* the Screenwriter Loophole.

I looked down at myself. I didn't look as sleek and tanned as the pretty publicists, but I didn't look quite as rumpled and dumpy as the journalists either.

*I'm starting to fit into this damn town,* I thought. *Who knew?*

Almost immediately, I recognized a familiar face across the lobby—an actor. What was his name? I couldn't remember. I knew he'd been on *Ugly Betty* at some point, and he had a new show now.

I crept toward him like a lion stalking a gazelle. He was by himself, looking around, probably for some publicist to tell him where to go. Or maybe he wasn't here for the junket. Maybe he'd come to the Hilton to meet his agent for lunch. He was wearing white skinny jeans and a pale blue button-down, untucked, and he was shorter than I expected, but he was definitely cute. He had a mop of brown hair, impressively jumbled, and I wondered exactly how long it had taken for him to get it to look so perfectly uncombed.

He'd stopped, so I stopped. I looked around, pretending I was momentarily lost, like I was maybe waiting for a friend. I pulled out my iPhone, pretending to text.

I couldn't resist glancing down at his ass.

It was a great ass, even what I could see of it under his untucked shirt.

*That ass has been on television*, I thought.

He turned for the restroom, but I wasn't about to follow him. That was too creepy even for me.

I turned and made another scan of the lobby, licking my proverbial lion chops. Where the hell was Jennifer Lawrence, who I just knew would want me to be her BFF if she ever met me by, say, bumping into me in the lobby of the Beverly Hilton?

A familiar face materialized right in front of me. Once again, it took me a second to remember who it was. There was something off about him. Was it the face? He was good-looking, but a lot older than I remembered.

"Oh!" I said. "You're Declan McConnell."

Talk about ghosts from the past! Back when I was in high school, my friends and I had volunteered to be extras in this zombie movie they'd been filming in town. It had turned out to be a terrible movie, but the experience itself had been pretty interesting. At one point, I'd even had a chance to talk to the star—Declan—for a few minutes, and he'd given me some good advice about high school.

Declan looked over at me, his face blurring in confusion.

"Sorry, you probably don't remember me," I said. "I was an extra on *Attack of the Soul-Sucking Brain Zombies*? You talked to me once and were really nice."

His eyes slowly found their focus.

"Shit, that was, like, five million years ago," he said.

I suddenly realized what was off about Declan Mc-Connell. It wasn't just his age. He wasn't dressed like everyone else in the lobby, like either the publicists *or* the journalists. He was dressed like he worked in the hotel, somewhere between a busboy and a bellhop. He had a stain on his shirt—something dark yellow that I hoped didn't smell as bad as it looked. Was he some kind of handyman?

"You're not here for the junket," I said stupidly.

"Nah," he said. "I work here at the hotel."

I didn't know what to say to that.

I thought back on what I knew about Declan's career. It's true that he wasn't a big star when they'd shot *Attack of Soul-Sucking Brain Zombies*. He had a supporting role on a sitcom, but it had been cancelled pretty quickly. He'd also been in a few smaller movies, although I couldn't think of any that he'd done since *Attack of the Soul-Sucking Brain Zombies*. After I talked to him on the set of the movie, I followed his career for a while. Did Twitter and Instagram even exist back then? I couldn't remember, but if they had, I would have followed him.

He'd been a rising star. He was even up for a role

as a superhero at one point. Deadpool? But that had ended up going to Ryan Reynolds.

I thought back to the time I'd talked to him on the set of that movie. He'd told me that even though he was still playing teenagers, he was actually twenty-eight years old. He hadn't really looked like a teenager, but he'd looked like a "movie teenager": younger than he really was, and also incredibly cute, which meant that nobody gave a rip about accuracy anyway. That had been eight years ago.

He wasn't young and cute anymore. You could tell he'd been hot—I guess he was *still* hot, for an ordinary, non-actor person, I mean. But now his skin sagged and had blotches, and his teeth were yellow. Even his posture was bad. If he looked five or six years younger than his years before, now he looked at least five or six years older. I couldn't help thinking: *At some point in the last eight years, he must have looked his exact age.* Was the day after that the moment when the twinkle had left his eye?

I'd been so awed by him before. Now it felt like I was talking to one of my dad's friends.

*What the hell happened?* I wanted to ask.

"What a piece of crap *that* turned out to be," Declan said, and I realized he was talking about the movie.

"Yeah, well," I said.

Declan glanced over at the bathroom. He looked desperate. At first I thought maybe he needed to pee, but this was a deeper, sadder kind of desperation.

This was like a scene from a movie: meeting a rising young star, and then years later running into him again, and he's not only not a star, he's working at a hotel and is maybe even some kind of junkie. In fact,

I think this *is* a scene from a movie, in the original *Fame*. And didn't something like this happen to Rachel on *Glee*? (I'd stopped watching by then.)

"So you're an actor too, huh?" Declan said to me. Now that he'd stepped closer, I realized he had bad breath. That figured.

"Me?" I said. I was still flattered that people some-times thought this. "No. Screenwriter."

"Yeah?" His eyes brightened—or as bright as they probably ever got these days. "Working on anything now?"

"Kinda sorta," I said.

"Really? You casting yet?" He was smiling his yel-low teeth at me when he said this, but it wasn't really a joke. He was actually asking me if I could maybe get him a role in my movie.

*Who would you play?* I thought. *The grandfather?* (I immediately felt bad for thinking this.)

"Oh?" I said. "You still act?" I hadn't wanted to ask, but I admit I was curious.

"Oh, yeah." He motioned around the lobby. "This is just temporary."

His eyes latched onto me again, like a drowning man who'd found a life preserver. "We should, like, get together."

There was a time when the idea of getting together with Declan McConnell would have literally blown my mind (and I know what "literally" means, and I literally mean "literally"). But that's when he'd been young and cute and a rising star, not when he was a desperate old handyman with bad breath and a yellow shit-stain on his shirt. The idea of *him* hitting *me* up for work was almost too much.

Meeting Declan really was like meeting a ghost

from the past. Anyway, he left a chill that was just that cold.

"Yeah," I said. "Maybe. But I'm meeting someone, so I should go, okay?"

He nodded, not quite getting my brush-off. "I'm done in a couple hours."

"Okay," I said, walking away. "See ya."

It was a little awkward, because I *wasn't* meeting anyone, and I couldn't leave the hotel yet either, not for another three hours. But I didn't linger in that lobby looking for any more celebrities. I spent the next three hours in a back corner of the hotel bar, trying hard to avoid Declan.

That night, there was a knock on our door.

"Daniel—" I said, opening it.

It wasn't Daniel. It was his older sister, Zoe.

"Is Daniel here?" she said, which really made no sense given that I just assumed he was knocking on our door. But I could hear fear in her voice.

"No," I said. "Why would he be here?"

She was anxious, squirmy, a body trapped inside its own skin. "He hasn't been home, not in days. I'm really worried." She stared at me. "Look, I don't know what was going on up here, and I don't care. But please tell me if he's here. I want to talk to him."

"He's not here," I said. "We haven't seen him. Do you want to come in?" I pulled the door open wider, in a gesture that was halfway between, "Come in, tell us all about it," and "If you don't believe he's not really here, you can come in and see for your damn self."

She brushed past me. She stepped around the apartment, even poked her head into the bathroom and the bedroom. I'd implicitly given her permission to look around, and she'd taken me up on it. (Once again, I worried about dirty underwear and bottles of lube, but then I remembered we had more important things to worry about than Zoe being shocked by the fact that Kevin and I had sex.)

"What's going on?" Kevin asked her.

She still fidgeted. "He hasn't come home, and he hasn't gone to school either. He won't answer his phone. I don't know where he is. He's never been gone this long."

There was a long, accusing pause. Sure enough, she faced us and said, "What's he been doing up here?"

I really didn't appreciate the tone. On the other hand, her brother was gone, and she was scared. I looked at Kevin. We didn't really know anything, but it was time to tell her what we did know, right?

"Well, he's been acting strange," Kevin said. "Ever since we moved in."

"Strange how?" she said, too quickly.

"Uh, friendly," he said, even though that wasn't really a good description. But I guess Zoe was smart enough to have some idea what had been going on, because she sort of stiffened in her shoes.

Should we tell her about Wednesday? I didn't know. If he'd been missing for "days," that must have been when he'd left. Were Kevin and I the reason why? But why? We hadn't done anything wrong. Anyway, we couldn't exactly say to her: Yeah, he came here and said he wanted to take a shower, but what he really wanted was to come out naked and show us his boner, so we'd take him into our bedroom and fuck him silly.

I remembered something.

"He mentioned a guy who said he could be a model," I said.

"What?" Zoe said. "*Who? When?*"

"It was a while ago," I said. "Wait. Did he turn eighteen last Sunday?"

Zoe nodded, wary.

"Then it was last week," I said.

*That's why he left,* I thought. *Not because of us, but because he'd finally turned eighteen.* Maybe that was also why he'd come on to us. Maybe the guy who'd asked him to "model" had come onto him first.

"Who was it?" Zoe said, still panicking. "You have to *tell* me!"

I thought back, but shook my head. "I'm sorry, I don't know. It was just an off-hand comment he made. I didn't really think about it."

The light in Zoe's eyes started to dim.

"I'm really sorry," I said. "Really."

She sagged ever-so-slightly. "I don't understand. Why would he just leave? Why wouldn't he at least *tell* me?"

I didn't know what to say. Everything I could think of was like a line from some bad movie, like, "Everything will be okay. You just need to be strong." Daniel was barely eighteen years old, and eighteen-year-olds are mostly morons. Still, if you couldn't save an eighteen-year-old from himself, there was something seriously wrong with the world.

"It's all my fault," she said. "He needs a man in his life. Someone to knock some sense into him."

This sounded vaguely homophobic, like Zoe was

blaming Daniel's confusion about his sexuality on the fact that he didn't have a strong male role model. Maybe that's not what she meant—maybe it was more about Daniel's annoying Tyler-Posey-gone-bad posturing. But even if it wasn't, it was still hard to judge Zoe. She was just a sister loving her little brother, wanting what was best for him.

"We'll look out for him," I said, and I really did hope there was something we could do. I still had no idea if Daniel was "a good kid," but I sure as hell didn't want anything bad happening to him.

I couldn't sleep again that night. It's funny how you can be so tired that you can barely sit upright during the day, barely stand to brush your teeth, but when it comes time to finally sleep, you climb into bed and your brain is instantly on high alert. It's like the night amplifies things—not just sounds outside your window, but also your thoughts. The silliest things, things you can ignore during the day, grow at night, becoming clanging gongs inside your brain.

I thought about Declan McConnell, and Gina and Regina, and even Daniel. Kevin was right about this damn city: there was desperation all around us, hanging in the air like smog. It was a little less visible on some days than others, but it was never gone completely. We were always inhaling it. To make it in this town, people here would walk barefoot across broken glass.

According to Kevin, my movie deal with Mr. Brander might not be real. So basically, he thought I should feel desperate too.

I was tired of it all. At that moment, I was also tired of lying on the futon, awake, turning and twitching, feeling every little itch in my underwear and t-shirt.

I climbed out of bed and went out into the front room. I could be twitchy and anxious just as easily on the couch.

As before, I didn't turn on the lights. I sat there in the dark, staring at the shadows on the floor and listening to the sounds of the city outside the open windows.

As always, cars whooshed by on the freeway.

Far away, a cat howled.

Something skittered in the dried leaves below our window—a raccoon or maybe a person out walking.

Was I alone in the front room? I couldn't help but remember the ghost of Cole Gordon. He hadn't spoken to me since that one night those months before, and that had been all in my mind anyway, a trick of the acoustics.

A floorboard creaked, probably the building settling. Then I remembered the building was more than sixty years old: wouldn't it already have done all the settling it was going to do? On the other hand, why would a ghost make the floorboards creak? Ghosts don't have any physical presence! (The association between ghosts and creaky floors has never made any sense to me.)

I didn't care. Right then, there was only one person in the whole world who knew exactly how I felt, and Cole Gordon was it.

*Whatever you do, don't—*

He'd told me that before, clearly a warning. If I really wanted to avoid ending up like Declan

McConnell, or Gina and Regina, or even Cole Gordon, I needed to not do something. But what?

"What did you mean?" I said to the empty room. "Whatever I do, don't do *what*?"

In the bathroom, the faucet dripped. Had it been dripping before, and I hadn't noticed? I'd been listening to the sounds of the night—the freeway, the leaves outside the window—and I didn't remember hearing the faucet dripping. Then again, maybe it had been dripping since Kevin and I moved in, dripping for so long that I didn't even hear it anymore.

I stood up and walked to the bathroom. I was still in my undies, and for a moment I was embarrassed that if the ghost of Cole Gordon did exist, he was seeing me like that. Then I realized that if he was real, he'd already seen me in far more compromising positions than this.

Moonlight lit up the glass block windows. It shone down on the wall near the tub.

There was something in that ray of moonlight: an irregularity in the wall, a small rectangle the size of an electrical socket. It had been plastered or spackled over at some point, and painted to match the rest of the bathroom. In the daylight, I'd never even noticed it before, but in the light of the moon, it was obvious.

There had once been an electrical outlet there, but it had been too close to the bathtub—it had probably violated building codes designed to prevent people from electrocuting themselves—so someone had sealed it up, probably decades ago.

*That's how he did it.*

Cole Gordon had plugged something into that outlet—a radio or a toaster—then gotten into the tub, and pulled the appliance into the water with him.

Cole's suicide was probably the reason why that socket had been sealed up in the first place, not some stupid building code.

The water dripped. The floor creaked ever so slightly—I swear it did.

Maybe this was all still in my mind. It probably was. I mean, ghosts? Come on.

I thought about that photo I'd seen of Cole Gordon. I'd imagined I saw fear in his eyes, that he somehow knew the demons were coming for him. He hadn't known then how to stop them, but maybe he did know now. Maybe that's what he'd been trying to tell me.

Would the demons come for me one day? They'd come for Declan McConnell, and Gina and Regina, and plenty of others in this City of Broken Dreams. Maybe they were right outside my door even now, waiting for the perfect moment to strike.

*This is crazy!* I thought. I was being totally melodramatic, as usual. The night had amplified my fears the way it had also been amplifying sounds, and my own thoughts. I didn't have anything to worry about. Things were going great for me! I was different from all those other people.

But maybe it didn't matter if the story of Cole Gordon was real. I knew the "demons" of the City of Broken Dreams existed, at least in some metaphorical sense. So maybe the warning was somehow real too, even if it was only a part of my own subconscious.

I turned the faucet, to try to stop it from dripping, and then I went back to bed. But it *didn't* stop dripping, and if the sound had always been there before and Kevin and I had never noticed it, now I couldn't get it out of my head. Eventually I got up and closed the door to the bedroom. That muffled the sound, but it didn't really help, because I knew it was still out there, never stopping, endlessly dripping on through the night.

# CHAPTER FOURTEEN

The next day, Saturday, Kevin and I took the subway downtown. Downtown L.A. is off most people's radar, but it's more interesting than you'd think. For example, there's the Grand Central Market, which is this old, bustling public market. We ate at this take-out place called Sarita's that sells pupusas: really thick corn tortillas—from El Salvador, I think—filled with cheese and meat and/or vegetables. They come with this little bag of pickled cabbage, which is surprisingly yummy.

After that, around mid-afternoon, I made a very small, very diplomatic request of Kevin.

"I'm leaving you unless you agree we can go visit a couple of different downtown movie locations," I said.

"Well, when you put it like *that,*" he said, "enjoy the rest of your life." He turned and started walking the other direction.

"Oh, come *on,*" I said. "We came all this way!"

He came back to me with a disarming grin. "Okay, lead on, McDummy."

I laughed. I'd slept like shit the night before, but I felt surprisingly good now—bright and alive.

I nodded to a nearby building. "Well, we definitely have to go into the Bradbury Building. It's where they filmed the final scenes in *Blade Runner*."

"I've never seen *Blade Runner*," Kevin said.

I stared at him. "Okay, now I really *am* leaving you."

Kevin rolled his eyes.

"Okay, okay," I said. "The movie itself is actually overrated. It's more the principle of the thing. It's just one of those movies you need to see. The production design basically created the whole 'dystopian' aesthetic."

Kevin smiled, and I knew when I was being patronized, but I didn't care.

Unfortunately, the lobby to the building was locked—there was some kind of renovation going on inside. We could only peer in through the windows in the door.

"See the iron railings?" I said. "And the open-cage elevator?"

"What else?" Kevin asked me, meaning, What other locations are you going to drag me to?

"Well, there's one other building, a couple of blocks from here. Let's see if you recognize it."

As we walked, Kevin asked me, "Just out of curiosity, you look all this up before we leave the house, right? I mean, it's not like you know this stuff off the top of your head."

I considered the question. "Little of column A, little of column B. What we're about to see, I confess I looked it up this morning when I knew we were coming downtown. But, I mean, the Bradbury

Building? *Blade Runner*? What idiot doesn't know about *that*?"

Kevin glared at me.

"Other than you, I mean," I said.

We finally reached our destination: a grimy building with an elaborately carved front and wrought-iron balconies. On the sidewalk across the street, I positioned Kevin so he was looking right at it.

"Okay, so guess the movie," I said.

"I have no idea," Kevin said.

"Oh, come on. It's obvious." When Kevin still didn't answer, I said, "*Minority Report!* This is the building where Tom Cruise hides from the little spider-probes?" It was even grungier-looking in the movie, and I wondered if they'd added the dirt with CGI.

Kevin turned to face me. "You didn't really expect me to get that, did you? You just like flaunting your knowledge of movie locations."

"Maybe a little," I said. "It's like you and sports. You say all these things like everyone is just supposed to *know* them, and I have no idea what you're talking about. I mean, end zone, dead zone, neutral zone? What *is* all that?"

"Russel?" a voice said.

I turned. It was the casting director from the movie project with Mr. Brander.

"Oh!" I said, but of course I couldn't remember his name. I felt bad that he knew my name, and I couldn't remember his. Now I had to try to fake my way through this little encounter.

"This is my boyfriend Kevin," I said. To Kevin, I said, "This is the casting director on *A Cup of Joe*."

"Hey," Kevin said, shaking the guy's hand, and I

was feeling pretty proud of myself that I'd at least gotten all the way through the introductions without referring to him by name.

The casting director laughed a little. "Well, I *was* the casting director."

"What?" I said, confused.

"Well, I mean, I'm out."

"What?" I said again. Obviously I hadn't heard any of this. "Since when? Why?"

"Mr. Brander didn't tell you? That figures."

My stomach was suddenly a black hole, so dense with gravity that even light couldn't escape.

I managed to say to him, "What didn't Mr. Brander tell me?"

"We're all out, Andrea, Justin, and me. We finally had enough."

"Enough of what?" I said.

"The bullshit, I guess. Bryce was sure right about him."

"About what? What bullshit? When did all this happen?" But I already knew part of the answer. I'd seen some of it myself.

"Oh, God, where to start?" the guy said. "I guess it's been going on since the beginning. I don't even know the whole story—I was just the casting director. Look, I don't want to tell you what to do, but you need to get the hell out. Brander's a crazy old man."

The black hole in my stomach? Somehow it was sucking my whole body in, so fast I didn't even feel the pain.

"Sorry to lay this on you all of a sudden," the casting director was saying, even as concern washed down his face. He looked at Kevin. "Is he going to be okay?"

"Yeah," Kevin said. "He's fine. Thanks for telling us. Nice to meet you."

I guess I'd suddenly gone sort of catatonic, but I saw the casting director walking away, giving me another concerned glance or two, and I felt Kevin pulling me down the street, toward something, I don't know what. What had we been doing? What city were we in again?

"Russel? Talk to me," I heard Kevin say to me, once we were underground, in the subway station, waiting for the red line to take us back to our apartment in Hollywood. "Tell me you're okay."

Finally, I managed to speak. "I need to call Mr. Brander." I fumbled for my phone. "I need to find out what's happening."

"Russel, maybe—"

"Damn it!" This far underground, there wasn't any reception.

I turned for the exit, but Kevin stopped me. "Come on, let's wait till we get home." I didn't want to wait, but the train was arriving, and somehow Kevin pulled me onto it.

I didn't say anything the whole ride back, just let the train jerk and jostle me.

When we were up out of the subway station again, Kevin said, "You can call him now."

"No," I said softly, evenly. "I'm going over there. I need to talk to him in person."

"Russel, I'm sorry. I tried to tell you."

I whipped back at him. "Really? Now?"

"I just meant—"

"I know what you meant! You were right all along, and I was an idiot."

"No, I—"

I started up the hill to our apartment.

"Russel!" Kevin called after me, but I ignored him. I was already running for our car.

I drove over to Mr. Brander's house. It was a Saturday, so the traffic on Sunset Boulevard wasn't actually that heavy, but I had somewhere to be, somewhere I needed to get to fast, and I couldn't believe how pokey everyone else was being.

An Infiniti hybrid stopped at an intersection right in front of me, even though it totally could've made the yellow light—and then I could've made the light after him.

"Oh, *please*," I muttered.

A black Tesla tried to pull out from a parking spot right in front of me, expecting me to stop for it.

I laid on the horn.

A Mazda convertible slowed to let a passenger out, but they hadn't even pulled over to the curb.

"Get out of the *fucking street*!" I yelled.

It wasn't until I was almost to Mr. Brander's house that I realized what I was doing—that I'd become an asshole driver just like everyone else in Los Angeles. When had that happened? I hadn't even noticed it.

I parked the car on the street, but I wasn't about to wait for anyone to buzz me in. I walked past the intercom right up to the gate itself. I jostled it some, but it didn't open, so I climbed over it and jumped down to the other side.

I walked straight to the front door, and I was on the verge of barging my way in. I had left my car behind, but I still had road rage.

The door opened before I could touch it.

Lewis peered out at me from the darkness, guarded, wary.

"What the hell is going on?" I said.

"You'll have to talk to Mr. Brander," he said. But to his credit, he opened the door wider and sort of nodded me toward the office.

I lowered my voice. I was still angry, but not necessarily at Lewis.

"Please," I said. "Just tell me what's going on."

I was standing there in the dark of that foyer, in that house made of wood and dust. My eyes still hadn't adjusted, but I could make out the whites of Lewis' eyes. They locked onto me.

"Russel, I'm really sorry," he said. "I wanted to tell you the truth. That first day when I overheard what you said about interracial casting? And not just that. You didn't deserve this. No one does. But, well, Mr. Brander pays me, so it didn't feel right. Plus, I'm a screenwriter too, and I really need this job."

Lewis was trying to make it as a screenwriter? Somehow this figured. I thought back to the night of the dinner party, when I'd thought Lewis had been trying to tell me he and Mr. Brander were a couple. That wasn't it, I realized. What had he wanted to say? What exactly was he trying to tell me now?

"He's done this before, hasn't he?" I said to Lewis, suddenly understanding. "Mr. Brander brings in a writer, tells him he's going to produce a movie based on his screenplay, gets them all excited. But it doesn't ever happen."

I don't know how I knew this, that this wasn't the first time Mr. Brander had done this. But I knew in my bones he had.

"How many times?" I asked.

Lewis hesitated. My eyes had adjusted at last, and I could see him clearly now.

"Three times before," he said. "Maybe more before I got here."

*It wasn't ever real,* I thought. *It had always seemed too good to be true, because it was.*

"So he just pretends to set up movie deals?" I said, angry again. "Why? Because he's old and doesn't want to be alone? He lures people out here with promises of fame and fortune? It makes him feel like he's still a player, like he's important?"

"I suppose so," Lewis said.

"Has he ever actually paid anyone?"

"Not for a while. But for what it's worth, he didn't lie. He never really lies, not to anyone except himself. He honestly always thinks the development money will come through. I guess that's how he keeps getting people to believe in him: because *he* believes. But he's had to work harder and harder each time. Even now, I think he still thinks he's going to make your movie. He also meant the things he said about your screenplay, that it really did speak to him. Out of all the screenplays he's read since I've been here, I think he really did like yours best. I liked it best too. Which is why I'm so sorry I never told you the truth."

I found Mr. Brander in his office, sitting at his desk. He was holding the phone in his lap—a landline.

"Oh!" he said, noticing me. "Russel, my boy! You're here. I'm glad. There's something I've been meaning to discuss with you."

I didn't say anything, just looked at him from the doorway. Was he finally going to tell me the truth?

"I have a proposal I wanted to run by you, and..." He stopped himself. "No, you're probably not interested. It's foolish. Never mind." He turned away, putting the phone back on his desk. I still didn't say anything, but finally he turned back to me. "No. I *will* tell you. It would be wrong of me not to. I think we've gotten to know each other well these past few months, and I consider you a friend. Do you consider me a friend?"

He looked at me, as if expecting me to agree. But I didn't give him any reaction at all, not even the smallest nod.

He smiled, a little bashfully. "I'm so glad," he said, as if I'd really responded to him. "And that's very sweet of you to say, my boy." He sat up taller in his wheelchair. "As you know, I make movies. It's what I do. It's what I've always done. It's made me wealthy, and it's made me famous. I'm proud of what I do. But of all the things I've ever done, I'm most proud of this movie I'm doing now. It's going to be big—I can feel it in my bones! People say that movies can't change the world? Of course they can! Of course they do. Those changes can be as small as when men stopped wearing t-shirts when they saw that Clark Gable didn't wear one in *It Happened One Night*. Or they can be as big as *Schindler's List* transforming our understanding of the Holocaust. But don't tell *me* that movies don't change the world!"

It didn't sound like Mr. Brander was telling me the truth, like he was finally coming clean. But I didn't stop him, not yet.

"But this isn't just about changing the world, my

boy," Mr. Brander went on. "It's about making money too. By all means! That's the beauty of this particular movie we're making: we can change the world *and* make money while we're doing it! But, of course, to make money, you first need to *spend* money. The earlier you invest, the more you make."

*This sounds like a pitch,* I thought. *Like Mr. Brander is trying to get me to invest in my own movie.* I was tempted to laugh, because let's face it, the idea that I had enough money to invest in anything was hilarious. Without Mr. Brander's option money, I wasn't even sure Kevin and I were going to be able to pay the rent.

But I didn't laugh. This whole situation was the opposite of funny.

"You've seen *My Big Fat Greek Wedding*, of course," Mr. Brander said. "Charming little movie. What you may not know is that everyone and their brother turned that project down. Everyone until Tom Hanks saw the project and decided he wanted to invest in it. They made it for five million dollars. Do you know how much money it ended up making? Over three hundred and sixty-five million!"

Even as Mr. Brander was talking, I was thinking: *My Big Fat Greek Wedding?* That was one of the most successful independent movies of all time, true. In fact, it was so wildly successful that it immediately inspired every investor in the world, and even the big movie studios, to start pouring whole shitloads of money into "smaller" movies like *My Big Fat Greek Wedding.* And then, in the years after that, everyone *lost* whole shitloads of money when they discovered that the success of *My Big Fat Greek Wedding* had been a total fluke—a weird combination of luck, timing, and who the hell knows what else. Anyone who knew anything at all about the history of independent movie-making knew this. But now here was Mr. Brander telling me that *A Cup of Joe* was going to be another *My Big Fat Greek Wedding*.

*He's not just pitching me to invest in my own movie,* I thought. *He thinks I'm a total idiot. He thinks I don't know* anything *about making movies.*

"Just imagine the profit on that, my boy!" Mr. Brander was saying. "Imagine how stupid all the people who turned that project down must feel!"

Or maybe this wasn't Mr. Brander's "idiot" pitch. Maybe it was his *actual* pitch, the one he and Lewis were supposedly making to investors. Maybe Mr. Brander really didn't know all the changes that had happened in indie movie-making over the last fifteen years. How would he? He hadn't made a movie since the 1980s.

*In other words, maybe Mr. Brander's the idiot.* No wonder no one was lining up to invest in our movie. Who'd he been pitching to anyway? Retirees in Palm Springs?

Otto had told me all about the Bullshit Factor—how everyone in this town lied about their careers by a factor of three. When we had that first development meeting here at Mr. Brander's house, I'd totally accounted for it: I assumed everyone was lying to me.

Everyone except Mr. Brander. I'd (mostly) believed everything he'd said. Which made sense, I guess. He was the one telling me what I most wanted to hear. But it was doubly ironic because he'd told us at that meeting, right after making his grand entrance, that everything that happened then would make perfect sense in retrospect. It totally did. Mr. Brander had lied about everything else, but he'd been right about that.

"I'm not one of those producers who is asking others to invest in something he's not putting his own money in," Mr. Brander was saying. "I'm putting my money where my mouth is. That's why I feel totally confident asking you—"

"Mr. Brander," I said, interrupting him.

"No, wait, my boy!" he said. "Just let me finish—"

"Mr. Brander, there's not going to be any movie."

He looked at me. At first I thought he was finally seeing me for what I was, that he was actually asking the stone-broke screenwriter for the money to make his own movie. But his eyes never found their focus. It was like watching a rock climber searching with his hands for a grip on a rock wall, looking for some kind of handhold, but never finding any. I guess there wasn't any to find. One way or another, he was going to fall.

*Mr. Brander is even crazier than the casting director said,* I thought.

"What?" he said softly.

"Mr. Brander, they've all left. The other producers? Andrea, Justin, and Evan?" Their names came to me easily now, even Evan, the casting director. At some point, the anger had drained out of me. What was the point?

Mr. Brander stared beyond me, his eyes still lost in the woods.

This is incredibly embarrassing, but even now some small part of me was thinking: *Maybe I can still work with him.* I mean, yes, he was a complete crackpot; he'd already alienated every other person on the project; and his pitch to investors was hackneyed and completely out-of-date, so he'd probably alienated all the possible investors too. But maybe I could still make it work! Maybe I could help him with his pitch, or maybe I could somehow even raise the money myself. Who knows, maybe Sally Field really *had* loved the script!

Thinking all this probably made *me* a crazy person. It had just been *so nice* to be able to say to people that I had a movie in development with Isaac Brander, the guy who'd made movies with Sean Connery and Sally Field, even if all three of them were older than God. For the first time in my life, it had felt like I mattered, like I could finally make a difference.

Just one small problem: it hadn't been real.

I looked down at my hand. I was clutching that signed copy of *The Glass Menagerie*, the gift Mr. Brander had given me at dinner the Saturday before. I must have left it in our car that night. I didn't remember picking it up earlier. Talk about having tricks in his pocket and things up his sleeve. Mr. Brander hadn't been wrong about that either.

I stepped into his office, just far enough to put the book down on one of the bureaus.

"What are you doing?" Mr. Brander said.

"Giving this back to you," I said.

He eyed it. "What? Why? That was a gift. I gave it to you."

"I know. But it's valuable to you, and it doesn't feel right for me to keep it now. Still, I appreciate everything you did. That you tried to set up the movie. And also that you had faith in me and my work in the first place. You're the first one who ever did, and that really means a lot to me. So thank you."

I turned to leave.

"Where are you going, my boy?"

"I'm leaving, Mr. Brander. I won't be coming back."

"I don't understand. Why not? What about our movie?" He sounded completely baffled, like he had no idea what was going on.

I looked back at him sadly.

"You're *wrong*!" he said. "There *will* be a movie! It'll be the best movie I ever made! The best, and the most successful! You'll see!"

Now I started walking away, out the room, down the hallway to the front door.

"Don't you walk out on me!" Mr. Brander said behind me. He must have rolled forward, after me, because a second later, he burst out into the hallway. "We have a contract! If you keep walking away, I'll sue you! Don't you think I won't! I once sued Katherine Hepburn—and I *won*."

This actually scared me, and I almost stopped. I mean, I was only twenty-four years old, and here was this guy, a former Hollywood producer, threatening to sue me. He was a crackpot, but I still didn't want to get sued. I couldn't *afford* to get sued.

I worked it through it in my mind: we'd signed a contract, yes, but Mr. Brander hadn't paid me. In other words, he hadn't honored the contract. I didn't know goat shit about the law, but I knew enough to know that you couldn't sue someone over a contract that hadn't been honored. And if he *did* want the screenplay so bad he was willing to sue me, well, he could have it. I could write other screenplays. It wasn't worth me spending more time around a crazy person.

By now, I'd reached the front door. Lewis was still standing there. I think he'd been there the whole time, listening. I was still mad at him for not telling me the truth, but it was hard to blame him. He'd been in an impossible position.

I nodded at him, and he nodded back.

In the hallway behind me, Mr. Brander said, "Don't you dare open the door! I mean it, if you leave now, you'll regret it!"

I opened the door, and I left, closing the door behind me.

It was well after dark by the time I got back to the apartment. The second I opened the door, Kevin said, "What happened?" It was like I could see the groove in the floor where he'd been pacing back and forth.

"It's over," I said. "Evan was right. Mr. Brander's crazy." I briefly told him what I'd learned.

"Oh, man," Kevin said. "I'm so sorry."

"But."

"But what?"

"Well, you told me so all along. Right? You were right and I was wrong."

"You think I'm *happy* I was right?"

"I don't know," I said. "Are you?"

"You're not being fair."

I wasn't being fair. In fact, I was being kind of a dick. But I couldn't help it. Los Angeles had been testing the hell out of me lately: not just that moment with Otto in his bedroom, and having Daniel try to seduce Kevin and me, but also the traffic, the smog, the noise, all the attitude from other people. I'd passed *those* tests (more or less).

This was different. It was one thing constantly being surrounded by the desperation of other people—of Otto, Gina, Regina, Daniel, Declan McConnell, and even Cole Gordon and Mr. Brander—to feel their dark emotion coating me like crude oil. It was another thing to realize that I'd been just as desperate as they were, even if I hadn't quite known it yet. And it was another thing still to realize that I was *right* to feel so desperate, that the things I thought were real weren't. I'd joked with Otto that first week that I was going to go barefoot in Los Angeles, but in a way, it had been true. And it wasn't just broken glass I was walking across. It was something even more painful. Yup, it was broken dreams—everyone else's and my own.

But so what? Bad things happened all the time in this town. I'd told Kevin that Los Angeles was the big-time, and it was, so what the hell am I moaning on about? All I can say is at that moment in time, I'd had all the desperation I could take. I said once before that I felt like an inflatable Santa slowly leaking air. Well, now I was completely deflated, an empty vinyl skin lying on the floor. I wasn't sure how I was even able to talk, but I was.

"You have no idea how hard this whole thing has been on me," I said to Kevin. "Writing movies is my dream."

"How hard it's been on *you*?" Kevin said. "Did it ever occur to you this has been hard on me too? In case you forgot, I had an actual career before coming to this town. I wasn't just a damn interview transcriptionist."

I had forgotten that. Kevin hadn't talked much about his new job. Maybe it was like how I hadn't wanted to talk about the movie project around him, how I was always worried what he'd think. He probably hadn't wanted to make me feel guilty, since coming to Los Angeles had been my idea in the first place.

Even so, I couldn't seem to stop arguing with him.

"It's not the same thing," I said. "That's just your job."

"And writing movies is some higher calling?" Kevin said. "Is that it?"

"That's not what I meant. I just meant this is a real disappointment for me, okay? Can you not let me feel *bad* about this for one single day?"

"Who said you can't feel bad?"

"You've just been *expecting* it," I said. "Right from the very beginning, you thought this movie was never going to happen."

"And that makes it my fault?"

"It's not your *fault*. It just doesn't feel very supportive."

"Supportive? You know how you just mentioned that I have an actual job? Can I point out that I'm the only one here who *does*?"

It went on like this for a bit, and I still couldn't seem to stop myself from saying things I knew I'd regret, and *not* saying all the things I knew I should. Why was I taking it out on Kevin? I didn't know, but somehow it was like a scene from a movie, the screenplay locked, and there couldn't be any deviations from the script.

Finally, Kevin said, "Just tell me one thing."

"What?" I said, impatient.

"Exactly how much are you willing to sacrifice to make it in this town?"

"What?" I said again.

"If you had to choose between me and making it as a screenwriter, which would you pick?" Now he was the impatient one.

What was I supposed to say? Kevin's question seemed totally unfair.

So I said, "I can't deal with this right now."

And then I went to bed.

# CHAPTER FIFTEEN

I was floating facedown in a swimming pool, completely motionless, dead to the world.

It was the next day, Sunday morning.

I know this is how this story started—with me floating in that pool the same way. But that had actually been pretty different. Back then, I'd been floating in that pool because I'd been so dead-tired from the move to Los Angeles.

Now I really did feel dead.

I'd never felt this way before. All my life, I'd heard people say, "I feel dead inside," but I hadn't known what they meant, not really. Now I did. It was different from having a black hole in your stomach or even feeling like a deflated Santa. It was like I didn't feel *anything*—like I didn't exist, like I wasn't even a person.

Like I was a ghost.

I'd woken that morning to find an email from Fiona. She'd finally gotten back to me:

**I've read your scripts. I'm afraid I'm not the right agent for you. Good luck. Fiona**

She hadn't said anything about Mr. Brander, but I figured she'd heard from him. He'd probably sent her an angry email the day before, or maybe made a furious phone call. Now Fiona, who had been stringing me along for months, knew there was absolutely no chance of the deal with Mr. Brander ever going forward, so she was cutting her losses.

I could not believe it. She hadn't even waited until Monday. That's Hollywood efficiency for you.

Kevin and I hadn't slept together the night before, not after our fight. He'd slept on the couch. That morning, before I could even tell him about that email from Fiona, he told me he was going to stay in Long Beach with his old college roommate for a day or two, that he needed some time to think.

I hadn't stopped him. I knew it had to do with our argument, and the question he'd asked me the night before, about my picking between him and screenwriting. But even if I had started the fight, that hadn't been a fair question, so I still hadn't answered it. Right then, he was up in the apartment packing up his computer, getting ready to go.

That was fine. I needed time to think too, or maybe just to see if I'd ever feel anything again.

Floating in that pool, I wondered if Fiona had even *read* my screenplays, or if she had just been waiting to see what happened with Mr. Brander. I wasn't sure which was worse: her reading them and not being impressed, or her not even bothering to read them at all and waiting to see how *A Cup of Joe* turned out—her whole determination of my worth as a writer depending on someone else in Hollywood liking me first.

This city made no sense to me, and it wasn't just the fact that the freeways all had different names. Mr. Brander had said the world desperately needed a story about gay love—not only what was awkward and pathetic and ironic about it, but also what was joyful and wonderful and real.

He was crazy, but when he'd said it, it had felt true.

But no one else thought so. No matter how convincing Mr. Brander had sounded, it had ended up being just another lie. My screenplay wasn't what the world needed. Or at least it wasn't what the world wanted. That was the worst part of this whole experience: finally feeling like I had something to say, something new and different, and then being told, "Oh, wait, never mind, not really, forget it."

I hung there in that pool, floating like just another dead leaf.

A shadow stretched out along the bottom. Someone was standing at the edge of the pool, watching me. This time, the legs weren't hairy—it wasn't Kevin. This time, the legs were black and were wearing what looked like Onitsuka Tigers.

Regina.

I lifted my head. I'd needed to take a breath anyway.

"Hey, there," she said. "I was hoping I'd run into you."

"Why?" I'd just lifted my head out of the pool, and there was still water running down my face, so I don't think she could tell what I was feeling, that I was dead inside.

"To say goodbye," she said. "Gina and I are leaving."

"What?" As the water ran out of my eyes, she became clearer in my vision.

"We're leaving. We've given our notice and everything."

"Where are you going?"

"We're not sure yet. Not staying in California—too expensive. Arizona maybe?"

I was confused. "You're *leaving*?"

She nodded. I worked my way to the edge of the pool where I could stand on the bottom, where I didn't have to dog-paddle.

"But what about—?" I said.

"Our careers?" she said, and I nodded. "I think we're going try something else for a while. Maybe run a bed and breakfast."

"A bed and breakfast?"

Regina nodded, and I had absolutely no idea what to say to that. Part of me thought she was joking. I was still dead inside, but I was curious too.

"Really," she said, somehow reading my thoughts. "We've given this a lot of thought, but we're done."

"Done? With what?"

"Our careers. Comedy. Screenwriting."

"But..."

"Yeah, I know. But we're just done. Really."

Even now, I was somehow assembling a pep talk in my mind, about how talented she and Gina both were, even though I'd never actually read any of Regina's scripts. They were so close, I'd say. They couldn't give up yet.

The words disappeared from my mouth before I could even speak them, like the water dripping down my face.

*They're giving up*, I thought.

I didn't know what to say. Everything I could think of sounded judgmental or patronizing: "That's too bad." Or, "Well, at least you tried." Giving up on a dream wasn't something you saw very often, in the movies or on TV, or even in real life. You saw plenty of people *achieving* their dreams: giving Oscar acceptance speeches, or winning gold medals at the Olympics, or being elected President of the United States. But not that many people accept Oscars, or win gold medals at the Olympics, or get elected President. So clearly a lot of people *do* give up their dreams at some point. I guess they mostly do it alone.

It was sinking in at last: Gina and Regina were what happened when someone's dream never came true.

Finally, I said, "Why now?"

"To tell the truth, it was you," she said.

"Me?"

"Do you remember that night we all went out to eat after Gina's show?"

I nodded.

"You sent Kevin a text," Regina said.

"What?" I said. Now I was really confused.

"Well, I should say you *thought* you sent Kevin a text. You wrote, 'Promise me we'll never be like Gina and Regina.'"

That did sound vaguely familiar. "But how—?"

"You and I had been texting earlier. I'd said where to meet me in the club. So you meant to send it to Kevin, but you really sent it to me."

"Oh. I'm sorry." I knew I should feel embarrassed, but I didn't, not now.

"Don't be," Regina said. "I wouldn't have told you if it was bad. It ended up being a really good thing."

I looked at her.

"The funny thing is," Regina said, "Gina and I used to *be* you and Kevin. We didn't just love each other, we *liked* each other. We never in a million years thought we'd become one of 'those' couples. But then you sent that text..."

My first response was to think, *Kevin and I are* nothing *like you and Gina!* But I thought about the argument he and I had had the night before. We'd been total jerks to each other (even though I'd started it).

Regina and Gina had once been us, and now Kevin and I were basically them. That was ironic. The night before, we'd even sort of sounded like them.

"It's not like I thought we were perfect," Regina said. "I knew Gina and I had problems. But that text was impossible to ignore. For the first time in a long time, I saw myself the way other people see us. So I showed it to Gina. Even before I'd said anything, she started crying."

I frowned.

"No, Russel, really, none of this is bad, not at all. We cried *together*, for the first time in years. Gina and I have been in crisis mode for twenty years now. It's always just one more pitch, one more audition, one more year. But it never is. It's like chasing mirages in a desert. It's not completely crazy—there really *are* oases in a desert, right? They're not *all* mirages. But there aren't very many of the damn things. After all these years, Gina and I never really found one. It was okay when the two of us were at least miserable together. But at some point, we turned on each other. Then we were miserable alone."

"So you're leaving the desert," I said.

Right then, Gina appeared behind Regina on the pool deck.

"Russel!" she said, a big smile on her face. She walked closer and stood arm-in-arm with Regina.

"I'm sorry to see you guys go," I said to the both of them.

"I told him," Regina said to Gina. "I told him everything."

They both kept smiling, beaming like the sun without smog.

"Be happy for us," Gina said. "This is a good thing. And we have you to thank for it."

"I am happy," I said. In theory. For them, anyway.

"Well, anyway," Regina said. "We just wanted to say goodbye."

"Goodbye, Russel," Gina said.

"Goodbye," I said, watching the two of them turn and walk away. They both had a spring in their step now they hadn't had before—a spring I'm not sure I'd seen since coming to Los Angeles. A walk like that was one of the first things this city killed.

I thought back to the night I'd mistakenly sent Regina that text. Could it really only have been three weeks ago? Since then, Kevin and I had ended up in a place a lot like them. How in the world had it happened so fast? It had taken Regina and Gina twenty years.

*And now he's leaving,* I thought.

But he'd be back. Wouldn't he? He'd said he would.

"*We'd break up if we ever treated each other like that.*" This was something else Kevin had said, that night we'd gone for that walk in Santa Monica.

I was still standing in the swimming pool, not

moving an inch, but suddenly I had one final vision of a different time and place. I was in Kevin's and my apartment, more than sixty years earlier.

*Cole Gordon faces his lover, a blond woman with a suitcase. She stands at the door, all ready to go.*

*"You're leaving because I'm a loser," Cole says to her. "Aren't you?"*

*"No," she says. "I'm leaving because you're not the person I fell in love with."*

*"I knew you'd leave eventually," Cole says bitterly.*

*She looks at him, so very sadly, as if he's just proved her point, then says, "Good luck," and turns to go.*

Had this scene really happened? It was probably like all the things I'd been imagining lately, all in my mind. But once again, it didn't really matter. Either way, it was true.

*Whatever you do, don't—* That's what Cole Gordon had warned me. Now I knew the rest of what he'd been trying to tell me:

*Whatever you do, don't let him walk out that door.*

Cole Gordon knew better than anyone what happened after they left you and your dreams didn't come true, what it meant to be truly desperate. How you could even end up one dark night in a very lonely bathtub.

I said at the very beginning I wasn't worried I'd come to Los Angeles and lose my soul, because I'd already seen all the movies about Hollywood, and I knew all the plot-lines. I hadn't lost my soul, but so what? I was about to lose Kevin, who was about a thousand times more important than any stupid soul. Except now that I thought about it, this was exactly how all those movies illustrated that the main character *had* lost their soul: by having their lover walk out on them.

Suddenly I realized I *did* have something to say, something really, really important, and it was even about gay love. But it wasn't the world I had to say it to.

I ran to up to our apartment and threw open the door.

"Kevin!" I said. "Stop! Don't go!" I looked around, in the bedroom, the kitchen, even the bathroom. "Kevin? Are you here?"

There was no one there. I was too late.

I wasn't feeling dead inside anymore. Now I was feeling like a fucking idiot. If I called him now, would he come back? Or had I really blown the one good thing I'd ever done in my entire life?

Behind me, a key jiggled in the lock, and the door opened.

I spun around.

Kevin stood in the doorway. "I forgot my foot cream," he said.

He started for the bedroom.

"Wait," I said. "Don't go."

He turned to look at me. I was still wet from the pool, dripping in the middle of the floor.

"I'm sorry," I said. "I was a total dick. I was disappointed by the movie deal, and I took it out on you. Of course I'd pick you over screenwriting—always, absolutely, no question, without a doubt. I love you, so there *is* no question. I don't know why I said those things last night, but it was stupid, and I'm really sorry."

He kept looking at me, and I didn't know what he was thinking.

Finally, he said, "It's all good, Russel. I said stupid things too. And that question? I love you too, so I shouldn't have made you choose. I'd never make you give up your dream. But I still think I need a day or two to clear my head. I'll be back, I promise."

He started for the door, leaving his foot cream behind.

"Please," I said. "Stay."

He stopped, facing away from me, standing in the doorway.

I wondered what to say. Did I tell him that the ghost in our apartment had warned me not to let him go, even for a couple of days? Or would that make me sound as crazy as Mr. Brander?

"I'm a moron, okay?" I said. "I came to this town to find my dream. But I already had my dream, and I didn't even know it."

He turned around to face me again.

"Oh, wait, did you think I was talking about *you*?" I said. "Oh, God, no! I meant my longstanding desire to take up skydiving. Sorry for the confusion!"

Kevin cracked a smile.

I smiled too. "Come on, that was some pretty cheesy dialogue. 'I already had my dream, and I didn't even know it'? I *am* a self-respecting screenwriter, you know."

He stepped out of the doorway into the apartment, toward me. "A damn good one."

"Eh, we'll see," I said, and we both leaned in for a kiss.

# CHAPTER SIXTEEN

Almost five months have gone by. It's the end of March now, and Kevin and I are still in Los Angeles. I've continued working on my screenplays, but I also got a job as a barista, like in *A Cup of Joe*. (Sometimes life imitates art, just like they say.)

Other stuff has happened too. I guess the second biggest news is that *Scarface*, Otto's web series, went viral. The first episode has something like eight hundred thousand views (and the last episode has almost that many, which means that once people start, they watch the whole series). A few weeks after it first went big, he got this incredible write-up in the *Los Angeles Times*. It was all about his life as an actor, how frustrating it was that people couldn't see beyond the scars. After that, Fiona made a deal with Hulu to start streaming *Scarface* (hardly any money—like, four thousand total—but good exposure, at least according to her).

Even better, casting directors all over town wanted him to come in and read. It didn't seem like anything had changed: Otto still had the same scars on his face, and they were just as distracting to audiences as before. But something *had* changed. He'd already been offered a supporting role in a TV movie, and he was up for this indie movie with Marissa Tomei. Maybe it was the web series, maybe it was the article, or maybe it was the two things working together, but now Otto is telling a story that people want to hear. Better still, they want to be part of his happy ending.

When we met for lunch last Friday—Chinese this time—he was really excited.

"What?" I said, before we'd even been brought menus. "What is it?"

"I got a sitcom."

"Are you kidding?"

"Hells to the no! I just found out this morning!"

"Oh, my God. Otto, that's fantastic!"

"It's not the lead or anything. But it's definitely supporting, not just reoccurring. It's set in a college dormitory. They're basing the character on me, on my experiences. They're going to interview me and everything. 'Course I have to sign all these documents saying they own everything I tell them."

"And it's absolutely definite?"

"Well, I mean, the pilot may not get picked up. But they're definitely going to pilot. And it looks really good. They don't shoot nearly as many pilots as they used to. And the script I saw is good, it really is. It's by one of the guys who did *Silicon Valley*—not Mike Judge, one of the others."

So the biggest obstacle to Otto's success—his scars—had turned out to be the very thing that helped him break through in the end. It feels like there's a lesson there, a really interesting one, but I'm not quite sure what it is yet.

As Otto talked, I tried to examine my feelings about his success. Was I jealous? Yeah, if I'm honest,

I was, a little. But if the City of Broken Dreams was finally going to grant happiness to someone, I was glad it was Otto. I don't know anyone who deserves success more than he does.

"If we're a hit, I'm going to try to get you a job as a writer," Otto said. "I already told them you were my uncredited co-writer on *Scarface*."

"Otto—"

"It's true! You gave me the whole idea."

"I did not." But secretly I was glad he was pushing for me.

After the waitress gave us menus and poured us tea, Otto asked, "So how's it going with you? What's going on with your movie?"

"There's really nothing new," I said.

At this moment, *A Cup of Joe* isn't completely dead. Mr. Brander never did sue me, or at least he hasn't yet. And a couple weeks after the falling out with him, I got an email from Justin. He told me that he really did like my screenplay (even if he also thought it needed work, even more than he let on in any of the production meetings with Mr. Brander). He and some friends had decided to try to put together an indie movie themselves, and they wanted it to be my screenplay.

The proposed budget is a lot smaller than what Mr. Brander was talking about, but it's not a micro-budget either. It's around six hundred thousand dollars, which means I have to be open to doing even *more* rewrites, cutting characters and locations in order to make it cheaper to film. On the other hand, this budget is a real one, not the result of the Bullshit Factor, or the figment of some delusional old man's imagination.

"It's going to happen for both of us," Otto said. "I know it is!"

I couldn't help but think back on that lunch we had right after I moved to town, when Otto told me how people really break into Hollywood, that it's a lot of little steps, combined with flat-out luck. That's exactly how it's working for Otto. For the first time in a long time, I'm thinking maybe it will work that way for me too.

As for Daniel, the news is less good. As far as I know, he never did come back to the apartment he shared with Zoe. Even worse, I was surfing around not long ago on my iPad mini (yes, I was looking at porn), and I saw a familiar, um, face.

Was this the kind of "modeling" the guy who'd talked to him had in mind all along? Either way, finding out that Daniel was doing porn was incredibly depressing. But it wasn't very surprising.

For the record, I didn't click on it (truly). Daniel is cute, and Kevin and I had shared a fleeting fantasy about him that one night, and I'd thought about him walking out of that shower a few times too.

But the idea of him doing porn was just about the least erotic thing imaginable. In fact, it made me feel ashamed about all the porn I watch in my life. Is that what the people who do porn are like in real life? Are they all desperate or confused? I know the porn stars themselves say no, at least if you believe their Twitter accounts and the interviews they give to various websites. But I bet a higher proportion of them are like Daniel than, say, the people who dress up like superheroes and pose for pictures with tourists at Universal CityWalk. How is Daniel going to keep from getting diseases? What's going to happen to him when he's too old for porn?

I showed Kevin what I'd found (and he had *absolutely* no interest in looking either). Then the question became: what did we tell Zoe? For one thing, I knew what she thought of gay people, or at least gay guys, and I didn't particularly want her knowing that we also looked at porn.

Finally, we decided she deserved to know, so we went down and knocked on her door.

She looked surprised to see us. And then suspicious.

"What is it?" she said.

"We were just wondering if you'd ever heard from Daniel," I said.

The suspicion turned to sadness on her face. "No. Nothing."

Kevin was about to say something when I noticed there were books open on her kitchen table behind us. They looked like textbooks.

"What's this?" I asked, nodding to the table. "Are you in school?"

Zoe glanced at the floor. "Oh, I'm just taking a course."

"Really? That's great."

"Something to distract me until Daniel comes home."

I couldn't be sure, but it sounded a little bit like Zoe was spending some of the money she'd saved for Daniel's education on herself. If he never came back at all, maybe she'd end up getting a whole degree. Who knows? After all these years of living her life for her little brother, maybe she'd finally start living it for herself.

Kevin and I looked at each other, and somehow we knew what we were each thinking.

I have absolutely no idea if we made the right decision, but we didn't tell Zoe about where we'd seen Daniel. I'm not sure we ever will.


Regina sent us a postcard of the Grand Canyon from Arizona. They could have emailed or texted us, or posted on my wall on Facebook. But there was something about a postcard that seemed so perfect, like they were on vacation in some distant far-away place, completely out of touch from the place Kevin and I were. Which they sort of were.

The postcard read:

**Dear Russel and Kevin: Turns out there's life outside of Los Angeles! Who knew? We couldn't be happier. (But we still wish you all the best in the world and hope to see Russel's name on a movie screen very soon!)**

**Much love, Regina and Gina**


Incidentally, I never heard anything else from the ghost of Cole Gordon, and I've never felt his presence again either. Assuming he ever existed at all, I have a feeling he's gone for good.

Somehow I also have this feeling I made him happy.

\* \* \*

The biggest news of the last five months? It happened just yesterday morning.

I was waiting for Kevin when he woke up.

"Get dressed," I said.

"What is it?" he said. "What's going on?"

"Nothing. Now I have a surprise for you."

"What is it?"

"Trust me, okay?"

Once in the car, we drove down Franklin, under the Hollywood Freeway, then took a left on Beachwood, heading up into the Hollywood Hills.

"I think I know what we're doing," Kevin said.

I smiled to myself.

Finally, we passed a metal gate and arrived at a dirt parking lot. It was early-ish on a weekday, so there weren't very many other cars.

There was a wide dirt trail—bigger than a normal trail, but not quite a gravel road—that wound its way into the hills, past the scrub and rocks. Unfortunately, it was completely covered with mounds of horse shit drying (and stinking) in the sun. It was seriously like walking through a field of landmines. I know Kevin saw it—he had to in order to avoid stepping in it— but he didn't say anything, which made me love him even more than I already did.

After a few minutes of hiking, the road rose, and the land beyond fell away, and we had this awesome view of the famous "Hollywood" sign, on the hill just across from us.

Now Kevin smiled.

We kept following the road, avoiding horse shit, up hills and switchbacks. Then the way split again, the road continuing off to the right, but a trail heading over to the left.

I led Kevin left, finally leaving all the shit behind.

We hiked along the trail now, winding between more hills and up switchbacks, always ultimately in the direction of the sign looming above us. It blazed white in the sun, and it felt a little like a lighthouse leading us on, directing us home. With each step, little by little, that sign grew larger. The sun was brighter now, hot. We were starting to sweat, and I was glad I'd brought bottled water.

The dirt trail met a road—paved, but long since abandoned, cracked and covered with rocks. Now we followed that road as it climbed ever higher. At some point, the Hollywood sign disappeared from view.

Finally, up ahead, the road turned left. There was a chain-link fence all along the right side of the road, but it's not like there was barbed wire on the top or anything.

I grabbed Kevin's hand, and we walked closer. Out beyond the fence, the whole city rolled out before us, hazy and sprawling, so vast it felt like you could see the curvature of the earth, even though they say that's impossible except from outer space. On the other side of that fence, down below us, the letters in the Hollywood sign towered upward. We were behind them, so we could see the metal scaffolding behind each of the individual letters. From below, the letters don't look that big, but up close, they're massive: each one is maybe fifty feet tall. Somehow we were the only people there.

Here's where I could tell you the whole story of the Hollywood sign, but you've probably already heard it. Besides, it has nothing to do with the Big News I mentioned before.

There were signs on the chain link fence that said *Restricted Entry: No Hiking Allowed to the Hollywood Sign.*

If this was the end of a screenplay I was writing, I'd probably have us ignore the sign and hop the fence, then climb up the scaffolding of one of the letters—maybe the "D" since it has the most room on top—and do the rest of this scene while sitting together looking down at the city. It'd make a great visual.

The truth is, people used to try to do that all the time, which is why there are motion detectors everywhere, and surveillance cameras on every single letter (with infrared for night viewing!), and even live microphones so the people watching can yell at you. They now take trespassing really, really seriously. If you climb over the fence, they immediately sense you, and they send helicopters to arrest you and issue you a massive fine (and also make you pay for the cost of the helicopters).

This doesn't have anything to do with my Big News either, but I think it's really interesting.

"What movie was filmed here?" Kevin said, staring down at the sights.

"Who cares?" I said.

He looked over at me, confused.

I got down on one knee and pulled a gold ring out of my pocket, and held it up to him. "Kevin Land," I said, "will you marry me?"

For a brief instant, he looked stunned. He'd expected us to come to the Hollywood sign, but he hadn't expected this, which is exactly what I'd wanted.

As for the ring itself, was it an engagement ring, or the wedding ring itself? Hell, I didn't know, but buying it and giving it to him then somehow felt really right.

His smile broke through the haze of his face.

"Oh, God, yes," he said. "You didn't even need to ask."

He pulled me up and planted one, way better than any perfect movie kiss, because it was real.

Los Angeles is such a Goddamn asshole. It's so fickle! It doesn't care whose dreams it breaks. Sure, it sometimes grants people's dreams. It has to do that, otherwise it would be a slot machine that never paid out, so people would eventually stop playing. And— let's face it—more than anyone I know, Otto really does deserve his success.

But for most people, most of the time, Los Angeles just shits all over you.

Still, if I've learned anything from my time spent in this asshole of a city, it's that you don't necessarily need to play by its rules. Sometimes you can take the pieces of your broken dreams and turn them into something else, something unexpected. I'd like to think Zoe will do that.

And at any point, you can give up the game completely. You can just get up and walk away, like Regina and Gina. I used to think there was some kind of shame in quitting, especially after working so hard and so long, but now I know that's not necessarily true. Asshole Los Angeles can break your dreams, but it sure as hell can't break *you*, not unless you let it.

Love is the other thing that asshole Los Angeles can't break. You have to be stupid enough to do that yourself.

Talk about your Hollywood endings! This one's the oldest in the book: like Dorothy and her ruby slippers, I had the thing I most needed right with me all along, I just didn't know it yet. I don't care if this particular ending has been done before, or if it's not cynical enough for modern audiences, or if the whole idea really is too cheesy. It's still the truth.

As I put the ring on Kevin's finger, he said, "When do you wanna do it?"

"Get married?" I said, and he nodded. "Why not this summer? We can rent out a bed and breakfast on Vashon Island for the weekend and invite all our friends."

"I love it," he said.

I'd bought a ring for myself, and Kevin saw it and put it on my finger too. The gold on our fingers blazed in the sun, leaving light trails like in some cool photograph.

Finally, we both turned and stood facing the back of the Hollywood sign and the endless city spread out before us. I was thinking about Kevin, and all that had happened to me in Los Angeles, and I'm totally realizing the irony even as I'm telling you this, but I can honestly say that in my entire life, I had never felt so fucking alive.

*The story continues in:*
The Road to Amazing,
*the tale of Russel and Kevin's crazy weekend wedding*

# ALSO BY BRENT HARTINGER

<u>The Otto Digmore Series</u>
(Adult Books)
\* *The Otto Digmore Difference* (Book 1)

<u>Russel Middlebrook: The Futon Years</u>
(Adult Books)
\* *The Thing I Didn't Know I Didn't Know* (Book 1)
\* *Barefoot in the City of Broken Dreams* (Book 2)
\* *The Road to Amazing* (Book 3)

<u>The Russel Middlebrook Series</u>
(Young Adult Books)
\* *Geography Club* (Book 1)
\* *The Order of the Poison Oak* (Book 2)
\* *Double Feature: Attack of the Soul-Sucking Brain Zombies/Bride of the Soul-Sucking Brain Zombies* (Book 3)
\* *The Elephant of Surprise* (Book 4)

<u>Other Books</u>
\* *Three Truths and a Lie*
\* *Shadow Walkers*
\* *Project Sweet Life*
\* *Grand & Humble*
\* *The Last Chance Texaco*

## ABOUT THE AUTHOR

Brent Hartinger is an author and screenwriter. *Geography Club*, the book in which Russel Middlebrook first appears (as a teenager), is also a successful stage play and a feature film co-starring Scott Bakula. It's now being adapted as a television series.

Brent's other books include the gay teen mystery/thriller *Three Truths and a Lie*, which was nominated for an Edgar Award.

As a screenwriter, Brent currently has four film projects in development.

In 1990, Brent helped found the world's third LGBT teen support group, in his hometown of Tacoma, Washington. In 2005, he co-founded the entertainment website AfterElton.com, which was sold to MTV/Via-com in 2006. He currently co-hosts a podcast called Media Carnivores from his home in Seattle, where he lives with his husband, writer Michael Jensen. Read more by and about Brent, or contact him at brenthartinger.com.

# ACKNOWLEDGEMENTS

Thanks, as always, to the holy trinity: my husband Michael Jensen, my editor Stephen Fraser, and my agent Jennifer De Chiara.

Thanks also to Philip Malaczewski for creating great book jackets, and Samuel Sebastià Holden Bramah for his terrific Spanish translations.

Early readers who generously contributed their time and extremely helpful opinions include Dori Butler, Allison Cassatta, Louis Flint Ceci, Ulysses Dietz, Nathan Edmonds, Neil Jackson, Crystal King, Bill Konigsberg, Darren LaFrance, Nate Leslie, Austin McCray, Kevin Miller, Peter Monn, Kevin Moser, Joel Mosqueira, Tim O'Leary, Megan Opperman, Robin Reardon, R.J. Seeley, Tristan Shout, Bret Tiderman, Gregory Taylor, Peter Wright, and Perie Wolford.

And yet another cheer for my assortment of creative genius friends: Tom Baer, Tim Cathersal, Lori Grant, Erik Hanberg, Marcy Rodenborn, James Venturini, and Sarah Warn.

CPSIA information can be obtained
at www.ICGtesting.com
Printed in the USA
LVHW04s1716240518
578391LV00003B/173/P

9 781514 382417